THE SURREAL ADVENTURES OF ANTHONY ZEN

CAMERON A. STRAUGHAN

Published by Kadath Press

Ontario, Canada

cameron_straughan@yahoo.com

www.cameronstraughan.com

Cover Art & Illustrations by
Pradipta Mukherjee

First Printing – July 25, 2022

ISBN: 978-0-9686981-1-2

"All worries and troubles have gone from my breast and I play joyfully far from the world. For a person of Zen, no limits exist. The blue sky must feel ashamed to be so small."
  Muso Soseki

"The streets are full of admirable craftsmen, but so few practical dreamers."
  Man Ray

"Humor is reason gone mad."
  Groucho Marx

ACKNOWLEDGEMENTS

Thanks to all the fellow writers and publishers who have given me support, advice and constructive criticism over the years.

I acknowledge the following publications in which some of the stories in this collection appeared previously: The Ontarion, The Peak, Drift, Exhibit B, The Dream People and Satire: The Journal of Contemporary Satire.

CONTENTS

Anthony Gets Up for Work

Anthony Zen awoke from troubled dreams. It was the loud ringing of his alarm clock that spared him this time. Rubbing his eyes, he was thankful the ordeal was over - at least until the next time he slept. The vivid imagery had been plaguing him for weeks. He remembered it all too well. It was the same each time.

There was a costume party at a massage parlour where men could get their trousers hand-washed without having to take them off. Anthony showed up wearing the banana costume his mother made for him. It seemed ideal at first, although it was difficult to move around in. It certainly got him noticed by the regular clientele. He felt proud. He was confident he'd win the prize for best costume. However, soon thereafter, a dark cloud rose on the horizon.

A man dressed up as Sigmund Freud arrived. He'd spot Anthony immediately and come running over. The dream quickly turned into nightmare. He just wouldn't leave Anthony alone. He took notes too! The nightmare always ended with the manager of the massage parlour approaching Anthony and telling him the costume party was last week.

Motionless on his bed, thoughts of troubled dreams dissolved, washed away by the annoying clamour of the alarm. He was fully awake now, yet he felt quite drowsy - a trait he inherited from his father. He pondered the day which lay spread out before him like twenty-four hours placed all in a row. Working and eating, eating and working - when would it end? The alarm clock, oblivious to such periods of deep philosophical thought, rang on insistently. This struck him as unusual.

While there's nothing extraordinary about being awakened by an alarm, or the fact it continues to ring until you make an effort to turn it off, he became so troubled he sat up in bed. After a period of careful thought and recollection, made almost impossible by the constant ringing, he realized he didn't own an alarm clock.

Pulling his covers over his head, Anthony assumed his cat was acting up on him again. Originally, he thought it best to take the cat back and get it fixed, but its guarantee expired long ago.

Regardless of the guarantee, however, he was honestly somewhat reluctant to get his cat fixed. After all, the eccentric feline provided hours of entertainment for friends and family. They loved to watch him sit atop Anthony's dresser, tail wagging violently, as he issued that strange ringing sound. For this very reason, and because he was his favourite actor, Anthony named his cat Monty.

To put it diplomatically, Anthony's friends never quite understood the line of logic that led to a ringing cat acquiring the name "Monty", but what else was new? Anthony liked to keep them guessing. Besides, who dares question the bond between a man and his pet? Ignoring the ringing, turning over in his bed, he considered his defence. To name something is to make it *personal* property; it is unique to that individual. While it is debatable whether or not a cat could actually be owned, his name suggested a great awakening – like the first time Anthony discovered Montgomery Clift. When you stumble upon something new and exciting, that you need to research thoroughly, you see the world with fresh eyes; you want to tell everyone about it. *That's* what Monty did for Anthony; he woke Anthony every morning to face the day with fresh eyes, to greet the world with happiness and optimism, spreading joy to all. A responsible adult, it suddenly occurred to Anthony what this was - poo poo. Free of further fantasies, his day was free to begin.

Anthony - not being much of a morning person - was rarely in the mood for Monty's early morning antics. He tossed a shoe at the ringing cat and chased it off his dresser, ending its annoying noise making. Luckily, Anthony always wore his shoes to bed as a defence against a wide variety of rowdy, ignorant animals producing strange mechanical noises during the early morning hours. However, the main reason he wore his shoes to bed had more to do with his amazing powers of forgetfulness - another trait he inherited from his father.

Anthony drew his attention away from his eccentric cat. He realized, to his horror, that it was 8:57 a.m. He had only three minutes to get ready and arrive at work. Empowered by a sudden sense of urgency, he leaped out of bed, got dressed, did his hair, ate breakfast and showered thoroughly. Feeling clean, yet incredibly wet, his mind began to drift.

Wandering around the flat, he found himself admiring his collection of round objects. Several of Anthony's friends had a special admiration for his collection. Every time an earthquake was threatening, they would race over to his flat to watch him scurry about, attempting to catch the round objects as they rolled off the high shelves - often crushing a spectator or two. It was all good fun and Anthony enjoyed it immensely.

Distracted by the collection of round objects, Anthony was definitely on a roll. He wandered over to his second-most prized possession - the answering machine next to his telephone. He stopped in front of the machine and asked it a question. As usual, it didn't answer. He decided to return it before its guarantee expired.

With some reluctance, Anthony continued to prepare for work. Monty leaped back up onto the dresser and rang on and on. While checking on the contents of his briefcase, Anthony paused to reflect on his cat.

Anthony's parents got him Monty to help pass the time. Monty spent most of his time atop the dresser – a small Buddha quietly witnessing Anthony's life unfold. Rarely did Monty move, except to twitch his whiskers. With each twitch of his whiskers, Anthony's whiskers grew longer. Anthony faced quite the dilemma – he liked being clean-shaven, but hated shaving. Such was life, he figured – and then there was the ringing. Anthony agreed with the old adage – cats never do what you want them to. Aside from the excessive ringing, coupled with some tail wagging for good measure, Monty *just watched*. Was he completely oblivious to Anthony's trials and tribulations? After all, Monty had the perfect life – sleeping, eating, chasing some leaves, sleeping, eating – while Anthony had to go to work; he could only chase leaves on weekends. Or was Monty secretly bearing witness to the minutia of Anthony's life? Second by second, minute by minute – Monty *watched*. It must be a heavy burden upon him, Anthony thought. All that watching, paying close attention to each and every moment, must surely keep the whiskers twitching.

Anthony glanced towards Monty. Perhaps he was projecting too much onto his pet, so much so that he was missing what was most important – the bond they had developed after years together. Their relationship was a geologist's dream. Yes,

Anthony knew it was a horrible cliché - but it was true. Resting on a solid foundation, the high peaks defied scrutiny. Occasional tremors shook loose debris. It tumbled down the slopes and gathered in the valleys where enquiring minds could sift through it. Cracks and crevices appeared and disappeared, challenging picks, hammers and trowels. Terminal moraines strove for significance but Anthony had already wrung the cliché dry without having to bring glacial action into it. It was time to put his thoughts to rest and finish getting ready for work. Anthony awoke the geologists from their dreams, gingerly navigating the equipment scattered across the floor of his flat. The geologists, never satisfied until they crack the hard outer shell to examine the soft magma flowing deep within, had a fit. They snatched up their equipment. With picks and trowels flailing madly overhead, dragging ropes and tents behind them, Anthony ignored their displeasure at being awakened and ushered them out the window. He watched them rappel to the street below. Casting off their ropes, they were madly off in all directions, looking for someone else's bedrock to examine.

Suddenly, Anthony became distracted. Sighing deeply, his train of thought broken, he gazed around the flat. Monty seemed to be ringing with exceptional vigour, for some unknown reason. It was just as well; he simply had to get ready for work, without further daydreams or drifting thoughts. With a new found sense of urgency, he completed checking on the contents of his briefcase. As usual, there was nothing in it. That's the way he liked it. It remained light weight - easy to carry, easy to keep tidy.

While making a few other last minute preparations, the increased ringing began to bother him. Peering out the window, just by chance, he noticed that several of his neighbours had gathered outside in their pyjamas, surrounded by their most precious belongings. They were nervous types, Anthony thought to himself. Monty's ringing rarely coincided with an actual fire.

Amongst the clamour, Anthony realized his door bell was ringing. It could have been ringing for quite some time. Obviously, Monty - having not been neutered yet - was greatly aroused by the sound of the door bell. This explained his sudden fervour. He was simply reciprocating the sound of his unseen mate. With hands clasped over his ears, Anthony rushed to answer the door. He was met by his parents, waiting impatiently in the corridor.

Anthony's mother was stomping her right foot. Over the years, this action had come to symbolize her impatience, although more than just a few keen observers had detected a direct relationship between the vigour of her stomping and the number of ants in her general vicinity. Regardless, her stomping motion was highly effective. The secret lay in her army boots. During grade school, Anthony suffered endless ridicule, because of his mother's choice of footwear.

Anthony's father, on the other hand, was completely naked. Apparently, he had forgotten, once again, to get dressed before going out. Yes, parent-teacher nights had always been a harrowing experience for young Anthony, particularly when the floor was covered with ants.

It was painfully obvious that Anthony's parents had dropped by for a quick visit. The note his mother took out and pinned to his chin - outlining their reasons for stopping by - accounted for most of the pain. Through force of habit, or by way of an excuse, Anthony checked his watch. He was overcome with panic. It was 8:58 a.m. He had a mere two minutes to get to work. Snatching his briefcase, he was left with no choice. Before his parents could get a word in edgewise, let alone demand the money he owed them, he thrust them into his flat, locking them in with his ringing cat.

Anthony bolted out of the block of flats. Passing quickly through the large crowd gathered outside, he assured neighbours and firemen alike that the building wasn't on fire. As he ran off into the distance, towards work, his father thrust his head out the window - apparently forgetting to open it first.

"Anthony," he hollered down, "you're not wearing any trousers!"

Like father, like son.

On the Way to Work

After running the first fifteen or so miles to work, Anthony Zen decided to pause and relax for a while. It had been a hectic commute - more so than usual. Pedestrian traffic was heavy and the city streets were clogged with motorists. While relaxing, Anthony peered into a reflective surface, provided by the numerous windows of a large high-rise. It was as good a time as any to check on his appearance. He was picky about his appearance. He liked to arrive at work looking his absolute best; it put him in a positive state of mind and increased his self-confidence. He was rather pleased with the mirror image before him. Although his age lay somewhere between thirteen and ninety-six, he could easily pass for either twenty-two or thirty-eight, depending on how frequently he bathed.

Anthony's youthful appearance was accentuated by his enormous mop of dark black hair. However, his hair often contained subtle hues of bright green, chartreuse and various other colours, depending on how frequently he bathed. He was thankful he had as much hair as he did. While running to work, he could expect nearly half of his hair to fall prey to the flocks of flying snapping turtles. The acrobatic reptilian pests plucked out strand after strand of hair, before returning to their nests atop a gigantic tower created to store all the money the government made from siphoning people's pensions.

Continuing to check his appearance, Anthony noticed - with some embarrassment - the bagginess of his underwear and the pale colour of his legs. The fact he had forgotten to wear his trousers did not dampen his spirits. He often arrived at work only to realise he wasn't wearing any trousers. He figured clothing was about the only element of his appearance that wasn't dependent on bathing. He could bathe all day long and it wouldn't help him remember to wear his trousers - and he'd probably miss work as well. Regardless, his fellow employees gradually got accustomed to his forgetful nature. After all, his trouserless condition wasn't nearly unusual as Barney Blackfeet's strange habit of wearing all his clothes backwards. Barney Blackfeet was even stranger still, since he wore nothing but long ball gowns - and his feet were actually black! Anthony figured that more frequent bathing would alleviate that problem.

It seemed like Anthony would never step away from the reflective surface. He had become quite preoccupied with his face. Something definitely wasn't right. He was clean shaven, and his complexion seemed fine, but he was troubled nonetheless. Of course, like anyone, he was familiar with the sight of his own face. He was naturally forced to view it during a variety of morning exercises, including brushing teeth and shaving, amongst other things. So it was not unusual that the smallest detail, the slightest thing wrong, should attract his attention. He didn't like to fuss with his appearance, but no normal person could ignore such a circumstance. Without hesitation, and without feeling the least bit frivolous, he carefully removed the note his mother had pinned to his chin back at his flat.

Embarrassed at his own forgetfulness, Anthony turned away from the reflective surface. After all, it was now 8:59 a.m. He still had another seventeen miles to jog, in order to arrive at work by nine o' clock sharp. He didn't mind jogging the thirty-two mile distance to work. It was excellent exercise; but more importantly, when he moved quickly through the pedestrian traffic, people tended not to notice the bagginess of his underwear.

Jogging along, Anthony became feverishly hungry. It occurred to him he hadn't had breakfast yet, due to extenuating circumstances and a lack of time. Luckily, there was an 'International House of Fish' just down the block. Approaching the establishment, he noticed a sign in the window: 'No Shirt, No Shoes, No Service'. He was relieved they didn't have a problem with no trousers!

Anthony entered the restaurant and promptly ordered a large salmon croissant to take away. Returning to the street with his order, he immediately regretted his decision. He realised how awkward the croissant was. It was shaped just like a salmon and it even smelt strongly of fish. Struggling to hang onto it, he knew it would only frustrate his efforts at getting to work on time. He expressed further concern when the breakfast delicacy suddenly sprang to life.

Anthony had no choice but to drop the writhing salmon croissant. It fell to the ground and began to flip about violently. Startled pedestrians screamed in terror and ran for cover. Suddenly, a N.S.C.T.F. (National Salmon Croissant Task Force) van raced to the scene. Four men, armed with spatulas and wearing croissant-proof vests, sprang from the vehicle. Anthony noticed that each member of the courageous task force - now converging on the agitated croissant - wore a large chef's hat with 'S.W.A.T.' written across it. They preferred using S.W.A.T. instead of N.S.C.T.F.; it was easier to fit on the hat and it looked more important.

Anthony instantly felt more comfortable in the presence of this elite task force - not because they were specially trained to deal with situations like the one at hand, but because they also weren't wearing any trousers. Like any government organization formed to serve the public, the N.S.C.T.F. was extremely forgetful. The four members of the task force began to wrestle with the floundering salmon croissant. However, they had to pause and ask for Anthony's assistance in subduing the vivacious breakfast delicacy. Apparently, their all-important fifth member was forced to stay in the van, since he had forgotten to wear both his trousers *and* his underwear. Anthony figured it must be getting close to 9:00 a.m. He politely declined to help restrain the rambunctious croissant and raced away, hoping to arrive at work on time.

Running along, he became increasingly aware of the sound of hooves behind him. Turning quickly, he encountered a large giraffe, following him closely. He didn't know what business the giraffe had on that side of town. Quite frankly, he found the situation rather startling. After all, the entire area had been designated a 'Giraffe-free Zone', following the brutal mauling of a young wheel-chair bound boy by an LSD-induced escapee from a giraffe retirement home.

It only takes one bad giraffe to ruin it for all the others, yet, with that aside, Anthony was fully aware that no giraffes *whatsoever* were allowed in that part of town. Conscious of the rules and regulations governing the city, and fully aware of his duty as a citizen to uphold these rules and regulations, he started giving the giraffe directions to the nearest Giraffe Relocation Office. He figured he was doing the giraffe a favour; if higher authorities became aware of such an infraction, the penalties would be strict. However, the giraffe, apparently insulted by Anthony's suggestion, reacted aggressively by seizing Anthony's long beard in its powerful jaws and hauling him up off the ground. The infuriated beast shook its head violently - back and forth, back and forth - sending Anthony flinging madly through the air, causing him to collide with trees, telephone poles and low-flying aircraft.

Anthony experienced a sudden rush of fear. He felt that his baggy underwear might catch in the wind and blow off, as the giraffe viciously whipped him about. He began to worry about the rumours that would surface if he perished in his present predicament. What a way to go - hanging partially naked from the jaws of an enraged giraffe! Anthony's father would probably understand, but his mother would never get over it.

Anthony was losing all hope of escape. The giraffe had an extremely tight grip on his long beard and it began to jump up and down in excited anticipation of the kill. Suddenly, something occurred to Anthony.

"Wait a minute," he thought aloud, "I don't have a beard!"

Anthony broke from the illusion, shook his head and carried on his way.

It wasn't long before Anthony was approaching the building he worked in. It was easy for him to find; above the front door was a large sign with 'WORK' printed across it. Just next to Anthony's place of work was an enormous clock tower. He glanced up at it, to see if he was victorious in his race against time.

Upon looking up at the clock tower, Anthony noticed the dwarf. The dwarf stood on the ledge of the clock face and continually moved the hands of the clock according to the time on his incredibly accurate wristwatch. The dwarf was about to move the big hand to the nine o' clock position, as Anthony raced towards the front door of the 'WORK' building. However, the dwarf - his strength weakened from his constant vigil atop the clock tower - was apparently having some trouble moving the big hand. He put all his weight into it. You could see the strained look on his face - even from far below. This was buying Anthony just enough time to further advance upon the front door, with the hopes of arriving at work on time.

Anthony raced up the stairs. The front door was just in front of him. A scream rang out. Anthony looked up, towards the clock tower, and saw the dwarf losing his balance. He couldn't move the big hand to the nine o' clock position after all. Anthony was at the front door, screaming with delight, as the dwarf plunged downwards and burst into a hundred pieces upon hitting the ground.

"It's not nine o' clock yet!" he shrieked excitedly. "I made it, I made it - I'm on time for work!"

Anthony turned the door knob. It was locked. He had forgotten it was a holiday.

One Day During Work

Anthony Zen arrived at work feeling confident. He kept confident tucked in his shirt pocket. Whenever he felt good about himself, he would feel him. Confident was small, round and furry. Anthony thought he looked like a ball of lint. Anthony's friends tried to convince him that confident really *was* just a ball of lint. But Anthony refused to belittle his little pocket friend by thinking of him in such a negative light. Anthony liked to feel confident. Just thinking about him made Anthony smile.

Besides feeling confident, Anthony was excited he had arrived at work at 9:00 a.m. Arriving on time always placed him in a positive state of mind. He calmly threaded his way through the glistening pillars, important looking people whisking by. He felt totally in control, on top of the world, as he climbed polished marble stairs. He passed through luxurious conference rooms full of velvet-cushioned furniture and rustic fire places. He entered a room which was large enough to get lost in - providing you weren't very bright. Its high ceiling was alive with frescos. Its walls were decorated with tainted glass windows that shot colourful light over the people seated in majestically carved benches.

Suddenly, Anthony felt strange. He checked his shirt pocket. His confidence was gone. He felt vulnerable. He felt alone. He felt like everyone was staring at him. He suddenly realised he'd forgotten to wear his trousers. To further the embarrassment, he realised that, quite by accident, he had entered a crowded church. Needless to say, Anthony was promptly led out by the ushers. Apparently, it was not considered proper etiquette to wear nothing but underwear while attending a service.

Outside of the church, Anthony turned and headed towards his proper place of work. The large 'WORK' sign above the door assured him he was heading in the right direction this time. He paused to look up at the clock tower; it was 9:01 a.m. He would be late for work after all. He noticed that the dwarf, who previously operated the hands of the clock, had been replaced by a tall thin man. The tall thin man wore a huge red wig. He tap danced on the ledge of the clock face, while tossing jelly beans down onto the street below.

Anthony stood and watched, as children gathered around to collect the jelly beans. When enough children had gathered, the tall thin man stopped tap dancing, pulled out a machine gun and shot them all dead. Once he ran out of targets, he put the machine gun away. He began his tap dancing routine again, except this time he threw down the odd chocolate bar, with the hopes of attracting bigger game. And bigger game is just what he got!

With the speed of a radioactive turtle, and a roar that would have knocked the socks off someone who wasn't wearing any shoes, an enormous hippopotamus raced onto the street. But he wasn't any ordinary hippo. He was wearing a blue tie and a large blue hat with a badge on the front. Yes, he was one of the merciless police hippos! He waddled to the scene because an incredible injustice had been committed - or maybe he just liked chocolate bars. By the time Anthony purchased the morning paper, enjoyed a quick cup of coffee and made an entry in his diary, the police hippo was ready to take action against the tall thin man.

Raising his fat head into the air, the police hippo let his demands be known.

"Bwwuuugggaaa!!" he roared, the incredible sound echoing throughout the city streets like a bomb blast.

When the phrase is translated from hippo, the demands are more clearly understood:

"Come out with your hands up. I have the building surrounded. You cannot escape. Regardless of whether or not you give yourself up peacefully, I will show no mercy to trash such as yourself."

Unfortunately, the police hippo could hardly see out from beneath his large brimmed hat. He inadvertently directed his demands towards the church, instead of the clock tower. As a result, three people within the church, all of whom understood hippo language, leaped off the tallest spire, preferring to take their own lives rather than face the fury of the merciless police hippo awaiting them outside. To Anthony's astonishment, one of the leaping people wasn't wearing any trousers.

"Hey, how come he was allowed into the church and I wasn't?" Anthony hollered, feeling cheated.

The tall thin man, still perched high up on the clock tower, pelted the police hippo with jelly beans, liquorice all-sorts, chocolate covered wafers and the most repellent of projectiles: fruit chews in the shape of famous newscasters. The hippo was infuriated beyond belief. He ran around frantically, trying to locate his aggressor from beneath his huge hat. In a fit of blind rage, he crushed two cars and accidentally ate three small children. But he still couldn't locate the exact source of the endless stream of confectionaries and insults regarding a hippo's lack of personal hygiene.

Help soon arrived for the enraged police hippo, who thought his personal hygiene was just as good - if not better - than anyone else on the force. A state-of-the-art police helicopter swooped down from the skies. It was outfitted with machine guns, rocket launchers, infrared scanners and computerized surveillance equipment. Now Anthony was really excited. He would get to see this magnificent justice machine in action. Now the tall thin man was really in trouble. Now he'd pay for his crimes.

Anthony wondered what specific action the police helicopter would take against the tall thin man. Would they just machine gun him to death? Would they fire some sort of high-tech net over him? Would they launch a couple of missiles, just to let him know they were onto him? Or would they just fly up to him and ask him to settle down? As it turned out, the police weren't thinking along the same lines as Anthony. They developed a completely different plan of action, in order to make justice more expedient and effective. Anthony watched in suspense and wonderment, as their complex plan unfolded before him.

The police helicopter swooped down to the police hippo. The side door of the helicopter slid open. An officer threw out a long length of frayed rope. The hippo clenched one end of the rope in his powerful jaws. The other end was promptly tied to one of the helicopter skids. The helicopter began to slowly rise, pulling the hippo up off the ground. The hippo held on tight, as the tall thin man sent down a shower of machine gun fire from his position atop the clock tower. Some of the bullets struck the helicopter and managed to chip the paint in a couple of spots. This angered the pilot.

The tall thin man soon ran out of bullets. With the help of

the helicopter, the suspended hippo converged on his quarry. Due to a lack of accuracy on the pilot's part, and partially due to sudden winds, the hippo kept swinging his bulk against the clock face, missing his intended target and sending a rain of debris and broken glass to the busy streets far below. The tall thin man ducked and darted, while trying to keep his balance on the ledge of the clock tower. In a wild panic, he punched and kicked at the hippo suspended before him. The hippo tried his best to hit back, but his stubby limbs were of little use.

During the intense battle, the hippo lost his policeman's hat. He was too busy trying to hold onto the rope with his mouth, while taking a few good swings at his adversary, to worry about his attire. Yet, it was a regrettable loss; it's difficult to find a policeman's hat that will fit a hippo. Even in his hatless state, the hippo fought valiantly. It was only a matter of time before the inevitable occurred. The tall thin man gave himself up. The long arm of the law - or in this case, its short, stubby limbs - had reached out and successfully dispensed justice once again.

Standing on the edge of the clock face, tears of exhaustion and guilt streaming down his face, the tall thin man admitted to his crimes. He demanded to be sent to jail. He promised to go through a lengthy rehabilitation program that would allow him to re-enter society as a gifted, caring individual. He wanted to make up for his crimes by devoting his life to helping all those he had hurt and becoming a born again Christian in the process. Before he could be arrested, he slipped on the ledge and plummeted to his death.

It was another job well done for the police hippo - complete with less paper work! However, the clock, apparently damaged during the battle, seemed stuck at 9:01 a.m. The hippo proceeded to further save the day by swinging his enormous thighs against the clock's large hand until it read 9:02 - the correct time.

Anthony cursed the police hippo for making him even later for work. Standing at the entrance to his workplace, he watched the helicopter clumsily drag the suspended hippo across rooftops, chimneys and antennas before it disappeared into the morning sky.

Anthony's Day Off

Anthony Zen was sprawled across the bed. He was completely naked, having just awakened from one of the best sleeps he'd ever had. He felt so satisfied - so energized. At the same time, however, he was reluctant to get out of bed. The soft covers were too friendly to part with, without feelings of remorse setting in. The comfortable mattress begged him to stay a while longer. The fluffy pillow further convinced him he'd be insane to leave, especially since he put three teeth under it with the hopes of collecting some fair coin, courtesy of the Tooth Fairy. The choice was simple - he would remain. He had just begun to fantasize about pretty young shoe store clerks, when his neighbour flew into the bedroom and told him to get the hell out of his flat before he called the police.

Anthony was too embarrassed to apologize, his neighbour seizing hold of him and dragging him to the door. Of course, this wasn't the first time he'd mistaken someone else's place for his own. Once he woke up in the middle of a crowded grocery store. When he demanded everyone leave so he could sleep, he was roughly escorted out by the police. His neighbour exercised a similar lack of understanding. Anthony soon found himself standing in the corridor, stark naked, the door slammed behind him.

Anthony had only himself to blame for his misfortune. He should have known he wasn't in his own flat by all the tell-tale signs: the absence of his ringing cat, which was indeed a delight; the enormous amount of food in the refrigerator, which he enjoyed immensely; the luxurious hot tub, which he relaxed in for well over an hour; and the mysterious people who kept giving him curious looks, who turned out to be his neighbour's wife and children.

Anthony was learning his lesson the hard way. He could imagine no fate worse than being completely naked in the corridor of a block of flats. As if things weren't bad enough, he completely forgot about the three teeth he had placed beneath the pillow. But he wasn't too concerned about that; they weren't his teeth anyway.

Anthony's main concern was getting all the way back to his flat, one floor up, without attracting undue attention. He thought about

'The Emperor's New Clothes', a favourite childhood story of his; it would be a convenient excuse. However, the emperor probably didn't live in a block of flats and rules concerning exposing yourself in public were probably more lax back then. Suddenly, he spotted the solution to his dilemma. There was a wooden barrel full of trousers outside of Mr. Aorta's flat.

Anthony rushed up to the barrel. He dug through the trousers like a man possessed. Clearing out all the trousers, he hopped into the barrel. Forcing his legs through the bottom, he pulled it up over himself. It proved to be a perfect fit. He couldn't ask for anything better. Of course, he ended up with a few slivers, but it was worth it. He was safe from any further embarrassment.

Feeling confident with his rustic wooden look, Anthony headed towards the stairwell, leading up to his flat. Carefully climbing the stairs, it struck him how fortunate it was that Mr. Aorta had left the barrel outside his door. However, considering Mr. Aorta's past, it was no real surprise. Mr. Aorta, considered by some to be the dullest man alive, used to stuff chimpanzees into the barrel, in a desperate attempt to prove that he was at least as fun as a barrel full of monkeys. He recently abandoned the practise when someone informed him the monkeys had to be alive.

Anthony was half way up the first set of stairs when, to his horror, he began to lose his balance. He couldn't reach out for support; his barrel would fall down, leaving him completely exposed in front of the stairwell security surveillance device, which consisted of an overweight forty-nine-year-old woman sitting on a wooden stool, shining her badge, adjusting her hat and slurping cup-o-soup while jotting things down in her log book. Anthony would rather not take that chance. He allowed himself to fall.

Anthony quickly realized that choosing to wear the barrel was a bad idea. He rolled down one flight of stairs, unable to stop. He tried to grasp the railing, but he was already moving too fast. He tried to cry for help, but he was too dizzy. After rolling down twenty-two flights of stairs, he became quite alarmed. His sense of alarm only increased when he remembered the block of flats had only three floors! Suddenly, he thought he heard a scream.

Sure enough, Anthony had accidentally run over old Mrs. Crowsfeet, who was returning to her flat after an afternoon of shopping. Continuing downward, he could hear Mrs. Crowsfeet singing 'Roll Out the Barrel' in a hysteric manner. Even with the world swirling around him - and plunging downward - Anthony couldn't help but smile while thinking of her. Mrs. Crowsfeet was quite the character. She definitely lived up to her name. In the spring of the year, she was often found perched up on the telephone lines. She also liked to nibble at dead things she found on the road. Sometimes she'd travel to the countryside, just to tease the cats, or chase the farmer's tractor. She was such a nuisance at times that the block of flats next door erected a likeness of Sid Vicious, just to keep her out of their small corn patch. But she spent most of her time knitting.

Anthony didn't spend too much time reflecting on his unusual neighbours. The fact that he was stark naked, inside of a wooden barrel rocketing downward to an uncertain fate, had been much on his mind as of late. He had no idea how many flights of stairs he had rolled down. There seemed to be no end in sight. He was losing hope. He thought of all the loved ones he'd be leaving behind. He wished he could go back and live each childhood moment to the fullest. He wished he could go back and ask the building superintendent to install an elevator.

Just when Anthony sensed death coming to his doorstep and making an appointment for sometime soon, his incredible ordeal ended. It took him a while to realize it, but he had come to a complete stop. Combating severe dizziness, he crawled out of the barrel. Surveying his surroundings, he discovered he was on a sun-splashed beach. Completely forgetting his nakedness, he stood up and stretched. The sun was glorious. The sand was warm beneath his feet. The pristine ocean beckoned to him. He stepped in dog shit.

Wiping his foot against the side of the barrel, Anthony heard someone approaching rapidly from behind. It was a lifeguard. He had zinc oxide all over his body, except for his nose. Anthony dove back into his barrel. He feared he had arrived - completely naked - at some sort of super exclusive beach front resort; now the lifeguard was going to charge him with trespassing.

"Hey you," the lifeguard hollered, sending a chill up Anthony's spine. "Can't you read the sign?"

Anthony peeked over the edge of his barrel, but he was too

frightened to read the sign. The lifeguard read it for him: "No barrels on the beach!"

Anthony Goes to the Arena

It was a beautiful day, as Anthony Zen strolled through the gates of the local arena. He was immediately greeted by the scent of popcorn and hot-dogs, coupled with the desperate cries of children begging their parents - or anyone's parents, for that matter - for the money needed to supply their fat and grease fix. The children ran circles around Anthony, laughing wildly, for no other reason than they were young, he guessed. He had no money to give them. Although flattered by their attention, Anthony was desperate to press on. The arena, jam-packed with people, was no place to remain idle.

Leaving the laughing children far behind, Anthony examined each and every queue. Tickets, souvenirs, bank machines, information, washrooms - a queue for every persuasion. Nobody was left out. That was the beauty of the arena - democracy in action. Of course, there were the notorious food queues, for the hardened veteran. The queue at the hot-dog stand seemed infinite and represented all age groups. The queue at the Brussels sprouts stand was curiously smaller; probably because the scent of Brussels sprouts didn't waft as far, intoxicating all those immediately entering the arena. Regardless, the Brussels sprouts vendors all winked and smiled as Anthony passed by. Some of them laughed out loud, which he found odd, since such good humour did not reflect their sales.

Edging through one queue after another, searching for the ticket window, Anthony found it ironic that at sporting events across the country, where athletic perfection and good health are celebrated and heralded, the unhealthiest foods imaginable are the most popular. And the humble Brussels sprouts vendor can hardly make a go of it!

Having successfully negotiated the throng of densely packed sports fans, Anthony spotted the ticket window. He approached confidently, having more than enough money to pay his admission. While purchasing his ticket, he couldn't help but notice the salesman looking him up and down. This was not merely imagined; he was leaning right out of the ticket booth. Anthony gave him a solemn stare that demanded he explain his strange interest. The salesman, noticing Anthony's displeasure, merely nodded approvingly.

"I like how your underwear complements your army boots,"

he shook his head. "That's quite the bold statement you've got going there."

Anthony looked down and, to his horror, he forgot once again to wear his trousers.

"Yes, of course," he began quickly, in defence of his situation. "My motto is: make a statement without saying a word. Good-bye now!"

Embarrassed about his appearance, yet proud of his army boots (like mother, like son), he raced over to the souvenir stand, to see if he could buy something to wear. He was in luck. The stand sold T-shirts, sweat shirts, hockey tape, shorts, joggers and jeans. Without the slightest hesitation, he purchased four rolls of black hockey tape. He wrapped the tape around his legs and thighs, creating an effect that, from a distance, looked surprisingly like a pair of trousers.

Anthony carefully waddled towards the rink. Any sudden movement would remove a great deal of hair from his legs, an excruciating experience indeed. Miraculously, he was able to reach the mob of screaming fans, but not without incident. At one point, his trousers became stuck to a large fat woman in such a compromising position that her husband saw fit to summon the usher. Problems aside, there was a growing sense of excitement and anticipation sweeping across the packed arena and Anthony felt very much a part of it. He was becoming edgy, volatile, ready to burst - but due to the fact his improvised trousers were too tight, more than anything.

Looking around the crowd of spectators, Anthony tried to pick his seat. But the usher raced over, telling him he wasn't allowed to scratch his bottom in public. Always willing to compromise, Anthony retreated to a dark corner where he could scratch his itchy trousers in complete privacy.

Anthony left his corner when the action began. The crowd went wild, the players pouring onto the ice. The referee explained the rules over the p.a. system. The game was called 'Dead as a Doornail' - named after the late fascist Italian dictator, Mussolini. The object was to kill as many people as you could and steal their wallets. It wasn't an easy sport, by any means. Not only must players combat each other using baseball bats while on ice skates, but two vicious rabid badgers were tied to everyone's waist as an added incentive.

Anthony tried to get as close to the rink as possible, but he definitely avoided the front row - anyone with any common sense did the same. The giant chickens ruled the front row. They sat there clucking away, with a lawless disregard for those around them. They were notorious trouble makers, often picking up rubber people in their beaks and tossing them onto the ice, causing the game to stop until the novelties were removed. Sometimes, a giant chicken would lean over the boards and bite the head off a passing player - a move that was sure to get any giant chicken barred from the arena for the rest of the season.

Maintaining a safe distance from the front row, Anthony still had a good view. The second period extravaganza was about to begin. Every year, one lucky contestant wins the chance to become 'Prey for a Day'. Accordingly, the contestant must don a red cape, wool socks and a neoprene rubber suit. Once suited up, he is tied to an enraged bull. The bull is let loose on the ice and, by association, so is the contestant. Enough time is given for the bull and the contestant to get to know each other and then the players return to the ice. The object of 'Prey for a Day' is to remain conscious for the entire second period. In order to do so, the contestant must avoid the player's bats and skates, while the bull familiarizes him with the entire rink. But the contest isn't merely restricted to the ice - don't get that idea! Should the bull decide to leap up into the audience, that's when the fun really began. If the contestant is successful, remaining alert and clinically alive throughout it all, then he gets to keep the red cape, wool socks and neoprene rubber suit - a handy addition to anyone's wardrobe.

To the dismay of true sports fans and giant chickens alike, the second period ended abruptly. The 'Prey for a Day' contestant had been successful. He was led out of the arena sporting his new wardrobe, while members of the audience helped arena officials search for his right arm. Maintenance personnel swarmed onto the ice and mopped up the blood, sweat and Lucozade.

Before the beginning of the third period, the audience erupted into a gigantic wave. Anthony wanted to participate, but his hockey tape trousers kept him glued to his seat. Forced to remain seated, all he could do to show his enthusiasm and support was violently shake his head, coupled with kicking outwards and throwing his arms up into the air. But the usher raced over, warning Anthony that whatever it was he was doing, it also wasn't permitted in a public place. Not wishing to be a problem, Anthony calmed himself. He watched the fat man in front of him toss popcorn to his two children, who were stuck to the adhesive fizzy drink residue on the arena floor.

Suddenly, Anthony realized that a flock of brightly coloured butterflies seemed to be attracted to his makeshift trousers. When they landed on his trousers, they became instantly stuck to them. Fluttering wildly, they could not pull away, yet others continued to flock to the same demise.

In a manner of seconds, Anthony's legs were completely covered with a colourful effervescence of butterflies. To his embarrassment, his butterfly laden trousers were drawing attention away from the crushing bones, spurting blood and screeching badgers that occupied the ice. To escape the ridicule of the crowd, he broke loose from his chair, leaving a piece of his trousers stuck behind, and headed away, searching for a toilet. All eyes seemed turned to him. With his flamboyant butterfly trousers, and buttocks partially exposed, he looked like mid-seventies Elton John!

Luckily, Anthony didn't have much trouble finding the men's toilet; it was the one with a penis painted on the door. The women's toilet was recognizable solely by the long queue of women outside of it. He was about to enter the men's toilet when the usher raced over and stopped him. Looking down at Anthony's trousers, the usher tried to direct him towards the women's toilet. Anthony explained his situation, inviting the usher to touch his trousers if he didn't believe him. The usher became infuriated by Anthony's insistence that he touch his trousers.

"Listen you," the usher fumed, "ever since you came in here you've caused me nothing but trouble! First, you make sexual advances towards a poor old woman in a public place - in front of her husband! Then I catch you openly scratching your ass in front of everyone."

Anthony remained speechless, looking down at his army boots.

"And as if that wasn't bad enough," the usher continued, "you were reaching orgasmic climax seated next to hundreds of fans. Now I've caught you prancing around in women's trousers asking people to touch you! Have you no shame?"

Before Anthony could utter a word in defence, the usher seized him by the collar and escorted him out of the arena. But

Anthony didn't think things were all that bad. After all, he often thought about starting a butterfly collection.

Anthony Expects Guests

Anthony Zen danced around his flat in eager anticipation of the arrival of his friends: Harry, Chubby and Jemmy. Full of joy, his feelings seemed to be reciprocated by his feline pet who rang on and off in an erratic manner. Monty's ring blended nicely with the eighties music blaring from a dusty set of wood finish speakers that date back to ... well, the eighties! The seventies were also represented by the sudden and unexpected inclusion of "Don't Fear the Reaper" - sound advice. Sensing a challenge, as soon as he heard the opening lyric "Come on baby, don't fear the reaper" Monty rang vigorously, proving once again that catbell trumps cowbell. The song faded into the distance and Anthony danced on, lost in his thoughts. A change in Monty's ring snapped him out of it. His friends were due to arrive any minute now. He had to compose himself. He had to dust off the speakers.

Anthony checked his watch. It was still there. He figured his friends would be arriving soon. Mere words couldn't express the excitement he felt, so he began to issue a series of grunts. However, he quickly put a stop to that. He was afraid that wayward pigs might begin to gather at his door. Impatience was getting the best of him. He checked his watch again. This time he actually made note of the time. It was 9:00 a.m. Yes, his friends would be arriving any minute now.

Having nothing to do with himself while waiting, and feeling rather unclean, Anthony decided to have a bath. He wanted to look presentable for his friends. Besides, if all his friends wanted to bathe, bathing before their arrival would mean one less person crowding the toilet.

Anthony began to fill the tub. The tub, which was quite large, once belonged to Anthony's father, who stored coconuts in it - not for lack of using it for bathing, however; he was just fond of coconuts. When his taste for coconuts waned, he gave the tub to Anthony to use as he saw fit. Anthony preferred to bathe in it. However, looking down into the swirling water rapidly filling the tub, Anthony had second thoughts. Did he really have time for a bath? What if he just slid into the bath, and got comfortable, when the buzzer rang, his friends waiting impatiently outside? He turned the taps off. Now he was in a quandary. To not bathe would waste a precious resource, still swirling below him. To bathe meant he'd be presentable for his guests. He picked up a skull that happened to be nearby.

"To bathe, or not to bathe: that is the question," Anthony began, pausing to reflect in the tub water. "Whether it is nobler in the mind to suffer the slings and arrows of outrageous body odour, or to wash your arms in a sea of bubbles, and by opposing stay dirty, I am dying to know. Maybe it is best to sleep on it; and by a sleep to say a nap. The heart-ache, and the thousand natural odours that flesh is heir to, are a consummation devoutly to be washed. To wash, to sleep. To sleep: perchance to dream. Aye, there's the rub; for if I rub off the dirt what dreams may come when I have shuffled the odour off this mortal coil? I give pause: there's the respect that makes calamity of so long life; for who would bear the whips and scorns of time, if you had to greet your guests either filthy dirty or soaking wet with a towel wrapped around you? What to do?" Monty rang and Anthony snapped out of it. The soliloquy was over; the solution was clear - he had to wash his face.

Anthony had a special face wash in mind, passed down from generation to generation. He prepared it with great care. Using the bath water (waste not, want not!) he tossed in a large bag of oatmeal. Traditionally, you were supposed to apply the mixture after waiting for it to set; it was recommended that the mixture be lukewarm and pasty. But he was in a rush today. Accordingly, he figured some motivational thinking was in order. He moved to the far side of the flat, in order to get a good run at the tub. With every muscle tensed - ready to snap - he visualized a race track, to psyche himself up. Several runners were gathered beside him. Two men stood side-by-side at the edge of the track. One held a starter's pistol above his head. The other held a microphone up to his mouth. Their eyes flashed back and forth - a secret code between them. They were carefully planning that explosive moment, yet trying to conceal exactly when that moment would occur. The tension amongst the gathered runners, including Anthony, was so thick that you could cut it with a knife - but you could never fit it into a toaster. Suddenly, the man with the starter's pistol flinched. He threw the pistol at the man with the microphone, bouncing it off his head.

"Go!" the man with the microphone screamed.

The race was on. Anthony bolted across the flat in record time, thrusting his dirty face into the tub. His hands were a blur, desperately rubbing the mixture up and down his face; it ran down his neck and stuck to his hair. He had to press on with it; his friends were due to arrive shortly. When he figured his face was finished, he towelled off. Standing, oatmeal still dripping into the tub below, he realised his clothing was encrusted with oatmeal. Glancing into the mirror, clumps of it hung in his hair. Every inch of him was covered with it. He rushed about frantically, tying to fix his appearance. He noticed he'd grown a long beard, probably because of all the worries associated with having guests over. Promptly shaving it off, he balled it up and tossed it at Monty, in a playful effort at frightening him. However, Anthony's little ball of whiskers failed to excite; he could not control his whiskers any more than he could control his cat. Monty merely twitched his whiskers, as Anthony's whiskers began to sprout anew. Soon he'd need to shave again. It was quite the dilemma – he liked being clean-shaven, but hated shaving. For Anthony, a beard signified calm acceptance of the inevitable march of time. It signified a return to a simpler life, closer to nature. It signified a gentle rebellion against societal norms. Unfortunately, for most people a beard signified hippies, unemployment and difficulty eating soup. And so, alas, Anthony would remain clean shaven as much as possible. Steadfast in his vigil, the cat rang on. Anthony shook from his thoughts and returned to the matters at hand.

Anthony combed the rapidly drying oatmeal out of his prestigious mop of hair. He took great pride in caring for his hair. It was as black as coal that had been immersed in oil for three years, baked in a kiln for two hours, cooled in a pot of black ink for one day, and allowed to dry, before being spray- painted black. When it came right down to it, however, he couldn't decide whether or not he should remove the encrusted oatmeal covering the rest of him. He remembered his Aunt Martha used to say that oatmeal was good for the skin. She actually wore it all the time. But then he remembered Aunt Martha was crossing a field one day when a pack of hunger-stricken Shetland ponies viciously attacked her. The authorities never did find her body.

Anthony quickly removed all the oatmeal. He didn't want to share a similar fate, especially with there being so many wild giraffes roaming the streets. Suddenly, his telephone meowed. He thought about getting it fixed, but it wasn't quite mating season for telephones; he could put up with its meowing until then. He did, however, go to the veterinarian's once to see if the telephone's meowing could be transplanted into Monty; then Monty would donate his ringing to the telephone. But the veterinarian, who communicated entirely by clapping his bare feet together, managed to convince Anthony that the operation would be too expensive. Besides, the veterinarian admitted to Anthony, in his own special roundabout way, that he knew nothing at all about cats. However, he knew everything there was to know about telephones. He had always dreamed of being either a communications expert or a switchboard operator.

The telephone meowed again. This time Anthony answered it, thinking it might be one of his soon-to-be-arriving friends.

"Hello," Anthony said, feeling rather unoriginal, yet lacking anything better to say.

"Boo," replied a voice on the other end of the line.

"Boo who?" Anthony demanded to know.

The person on the other end of the line broke into hysterical laughter.

"Why are you so sad?" the caller finally forced a response, between cries of laughter.

Anthony knew right away it was his mother. She enjoyed executing a prank call almost as much as she enjoyed receiving one. She particularly enjoyed calling up the neighbourhood children and asking if their parents were home. If the children proved to be alone in the house, she'd tell them that she saw Bigfoot climbing up onto their roof and disappearing down their chimney. But today Anthony's mother had phoned, on behalf of his father, to remind him that he was supposed to go out for dinner with them tomorrow. She began to go on about old Mrs. Crabtree's gall bladder infection, which stopped her from participating in last Sunday's Tupperware party, when Anthony made a clever excuse to get her off the phone without seeming rude. He told her he just heard something big climb up onto his roof and it seemed to be coming down his chimney.

With Mother off the telephone, Anthony continued to prepare for the arrival of his friends. He was beginning to wonder whatever happened to them, when his telephone meowed again. Reluctant to answer, he feared his friends weren't coming after all. The telephone continued to meow. How he hated the constant meowing! But he was glad he didn't have a telephone like Harry's. Every time a call came through, Harry's telephone made a noise like an ocean perch. Since an ocean perch isn't capable of making an audible sound, aside from a bit of tail flapping, Harry missed just about all his calls.

With some hesitation, Anthony moved to answer his telephone. His cat suddenly began to ring with exceptional vigour, apparently jealous of how much attention Anthony was paying to the telephone. Anthony picked up the receiver.

"Hello," he said sternly.

"Your dog is in my garden," a voice announced, with an overly obvious southern accent.

"I don't have a dog," Anthony replied impatiently.

"Neither do I!" the caller roared.

Anthony listened to a moment of wild laughter, followed by a period of silence. He thought he could hear someone whispering instructions to the caller.

"I mean," the caller came back on, southern accent still intact, "well, I don't have a garden!"

The wild laughter began anew. Anthony quickly figured out who it was; the phoney southern accent was a dead giveaway. It was his friend, Harry, and his accomplice, Chubby. Harry enjoyed executing a prank call almost as much as he enjoyed receiving one. He particularly enjoyed calling up the neighbourhood children and asking if their parents were home. If the children proved to be alone in the house, he'd tell them he saw Bear Grylls climbing up onto their roof and disappearing down their chimney. But today Anthony's good friend had called on behalf of himself, Chubby and Jemmy to inform him they weren't coming over after all. Apparently, they all decided to stay at home and watch television. Harry began to go on about old Mrs. Crabtree's gall bladder infection, which stopped her from participating in last Sunday's football match, when Anthony made an excuse to get him off the phone without seeming rude. Anthony told him he just heard something big climb up onto his roof and it seemed to be coming down his chimney.

Hanging up the telephone, Anthony was upset, to say the least. He didn't like it when plans fell apart. He was particularly bothered by Harry's insensitive, immature nature. Under the circumstances, it was improper for Harry to play pranks. Besides, what right did Harry have to torment people with cruel jokes when his family name was Balls? Worst still, he always hung around a guy named Chubby!

To relieve his boredom, Anthony switched on the television. There wasn't much on. Bear Grylls had a special in which he investigated Bigfoot sightings on urban rooftops, but that was about it. Anthony checked his watch; it was 9:01 a.m. He still had the entire day to use as he saw fit. Turning off the television, he considered his options. He had speakers to dust off and a tub full of rapidly cooling oatmeal. Cranking up the eighties, he shaved his beard. Monty rang on approvingly. Peering over the edge of the tub, he studied the murky waters, barely capturing his reflection. Did he have time to bathe? He picked up a skull that happened to be nearby.

"To bathe, or not to bathe: that is the question," Anthony began. "Whether it is nobler in the mind to suffer the slings and arrows ..."

Anthony at Work

It was 9:01 a.m. and Anthony Zen couldn't recall ever being so busy. Seated behind his desk, he had been diligently sharpening pencils, shuffling papers, emptying pencil sharpeners, cleaning out his bin, sharpening more pencils and emptying more pencil sharpeners. Now it was finally time for his break.

Anthony enjoyed his break almost as much as he enjoyed sharpening pencils and shuffling papers. However, he debated whether or not to make it a short break; after all, he spent the better part of the morning sharpening pencils and he still had a lot of papers to shuffle. Nevertheless, after quite some thought, he was convinced that a longer break was needed. His reasoning was flawless. Since he began work promptly at 9:00 a.m., and already accomplished enough pencil sharpening to make up for a lack of paper shuffling, a longer break was definitely in order.

Anthony began his break by wandering over to Meathead's desk. Meathead was busy sniffing Liquid Paper. Meathead never took breaks, but he never really worked either. Anthony heard rumours that Meathead never went home after work. He remained seated at his desk, sniffing Liquid Paper, twenty-four hours a day. However, Meathead wasn't always seated at his desk; quite often, he'd be floating several feet above it. If you approached him, trying to convince him of the possible side effects of sniffing Liquid Paper, he'd only invite you to scratch his stomach. Sometimes, just for fun, someone would turn on the ceiling fans and everyone would gather to watch Meathead float around the office. Unfortunately, there was always some cruel individual who'd open a window - perhaps accidentally. Meathead would drift out, get caught in a good wind and no one would hear from him for weeks on end.

The boss didn't like it when Meathead drifted away. Meathead was his favourite employee; why shouldn't he be? After all, Meathead was a man of simple needs. He didn't need to be supplied with pencils to be sharpened, or papers to shuffle - he didn't even need a pay cheque! He was happy, as long as there was Liquid Paper to sniff.

Anthony decided to spend his break talking to Meathead.

Meathead was a rather interesting fellow. During his excessive vacation time, he'd travel to any factory that produced nail polish, rubber tyres, or model glue. He liked to go wherever he could inhale deeply and get a cheap high.

"What's it like - travelling all over the country, smelling things?" Anthony asked.

"Down at the supermarket, you can buy huge quantities of bacon," Meathead replied. "Then you fry it up and serve it with a roast turkey."

Meathead was a man who lived up to his name. You could always get a straight answer out of him, provided you wanted to talk about meat. Quickly realizing his mistake, Anthony decided to avoid Meathead and use his break for other activities. But it was too late. Meathead grabbed hold of his arm and began to lecture.

"Did you know that vegetables are bad for you?" Meathead began. "Well, they are! You should eat lots of raw hamburger!"

"Meathead, I think Liquid Paper has ruined your life," Anthony confessed, pausing for a proper psychological term to describe Meathead's condition. "You're ... you're ... you're a stupid dummy!"

"Would you like a slice of smoked ham?" Meathead retorted.

Anthony pulled away from Meathead's carnivorous influence. He decided to visit with Miss Java, whose desk was covered with steaming kettles and various pots.

"Could I borrow a paper-clip?" he asked, intending to start a stimulating conversation.

"Would you like a cup of coffee?" Miss Java smiled, as if oblivious to the request.

"No thanks. Just a paper-clip."

"How about two cups?"

"No, no," Anthony shook his head, "I don't want any coffee at all - just a paper-clip."

"Well then," Miss Java paused, "how about some tea or cappuccino?"

"I don't want anything to drink!" Anthony burst, jumping up and down, pulling on his hair. "All I want is a paper-clip! Why can't you understand that? Why am I wasting my break getting red in the face? I might as well be sharpening pencils and shuffling papers!"

"You seem tense," Miss Java observed. "Maybe you should

try some decaffeinated."

"No, I shouldn't," Anthony leaned over her desk, having calmed down somewhat. "Since when is a hot beverage a prerequisite for a paper-clip? Besides, I didn't need a paper-clip in the first place. I was just trying to stimulate conversation and make the most of my break. But I definitely didn't come over here for coffee."

Anthony paused to see Miss Java's reaction to his plea. He hoped she would understand his desperate situation. She seemed to be deep in thought. Sitting forward, she motioned for him to lean in closer. He was both curious and excited; there was no telling what she had to say, but most likely it was important - maybe even personal.

"Coffee beans come from Columbia," she began without shame. "They're picked fresh daily by a Mexican-looking guy and his donkey. But donkeys can't pick coffee beans by themselves!"

Miss Java, expecting to finish her lecture, looked everywhere for Anthony, to no avail. He was hiding under his desk; he raced beneath it, shortly after the words 'coffee beans' left her lips. He was extremely upset, to say the least. The only conversation he could generate during his break had to revolve around either meat or coffee. He felt like remaining hidden for the rest of the day.

Realizing his break was over, Anthony got back to work. He was in the midst of some serious paper shuffling, when he heard his boss calling for him. Anthony hated his boss. The man was a pig. He had a fat, round nose; pointy ears; beady little eyes; pink skin; a curly tail; and he smelled like bacon - Meathead liked that smell, but no one else did.

Reluctantly, Anthony entered the boss's office. The walls were decorated with high school mud-wrestling awards. The boss didn't acknowledge Anthony's presence; he had his head out the window, apparently preoccupied with something on the street below. Anthony had no idea why he was summoned. Perhaps the fact his boss chose not to face him meant bad news. Maybe he was ignoring Anthony to intimidate him, to scare him into sharpening pencils and shuffling papers with more efficiency. It was working; Anthony felt uncomfortable - even guilty. He began to expect the worst.

"I see a sausage vendor!" the boss suddenly screeched, causing Anthony to jump. "It's an atrocity," he continued, pulling his head inside and turning to Anthony- "shouldn't be allowed. I hate meat; it's disloyal! Did you know that meat is bad for you?" he pointed at Anthony, without pausing for his reply. "Well, it is! You should eat lots of raw turnip!"

Once again, misfortune paid an unwanted visit to Anthony. He couldn't just up and leave his boss's office; it wasn't as easy as avoiding Meathead and Miss Java. Now he'd have to put up with yet another lecture.

"Fresh vegetables are the best," the boss began, in the most prestigious manner possible, for a man who resembled a pig. "You should clean them before eating them - dirt is for rolling in, not for eating!"

"I've got a lot of paper shuffling to do," Anthony tried to slip away, "I'd better get back to it."

"Turnips are grown in Kentucky," the boss continued, regardless. "They're picked fresh daily by a Southern-looking guy and his donkey. But donkeys can't pick turnips by themselves!"

By now, Anthony was accustomed to hiding under his desk; in fact, he raced beneath it in record time. Remaining completely silent, he could still hear his boss pacing around the office, lecturing about vegetables, apparently unaware that Anthony was no longer present. However, it wasn't long before the lecturing stopped. Shortly thereafter, Anthony heard the sign - something large falling to the floor. His boss fell asleep on his feet again. Now it was safe for Anthony to come out from hiding.

In an effort to look busy, Anthony shuffled a few more papers and sharpened a few more pencils. To greatly increase his chances of appearing busy, he got a firm hold on a rubber. He rubbed it back and forth, back and forth across the papers sprawled out in front of him. Then he spent an inordinate amount of time trying to coax the little pieces of pink rubber off his desk and clothes.

Anthony soon succumbed to his favourite pastime - he checked his watch. It was 9:01 a.m. Time seemed to be dragging, so he decided to watch Meathead and Miss Java argue over which was better - meat or coffee. Events unfolded in the usual fashion. Seated at their respective desks, Meathead and Miss Java began with a civilized debate, each of them presenting their arguments in a calm, collected manner. However, it wasn't long before Meathead began throwing sausage rolls. Miss Java retaliated with a barrage of coffee beans. No one could guess what straw broke the camel's back, but the air was alive with projectile luncheon meat and exotic coffee beans. The boss leaped into the fray, throwing turnips.

Of course, the boss eventually won the argument; turnips are quite heavy, knocking both Meathead and Miss Java unconscious upon hitting them. Surveying the scene of his victory, the boss cleared his throat, preparing to make a speech.

"Meat and coffee are both bad for your health," he began, in a manner reminiscent of Winston Churchill. "Turnips, however, are an excellent source of vitamins and they're easy to throw. Always bring some to a fight!"

Anthony became quite nervous. His boss stopped talking, picked up a turnip and started approaching him. Anthony considered hiding beneath his desk; it was quickly becoming his favourite haunt. But his boss was already well within striking distance.

"Anthony!" the boss hollered.

Anthony feared the worst.

"Anthony!" the boss held up the turnip. "I want you to have this turnip for your collection of round objects."

Anthony issued a sigh of relief.

"And you've done such a good job of sharpening pencils and shuffling papers," the boss quickly added, "that I'm going to give you the rest of the day off, with no pay for the next three weeks."

Anthony thanked the boss for his generosity. Although things started off on the wrong foot, it turned out to be a good day after all. Excited as ever, free from his laborious duties, he ran the thirty-two mile distance home and added the turnip to his collection of round objects.

Anthony Goes out for Dinner with His Parents

In life, there are those who lead and those who follow. And then there are those who stay at home and eat pies. Anthony Zen was one of the latter. He was a pie eater - and proud of it. However, there didn't seem to be enough hours in the day for pie eating. He had just dug into his third pie when the telephone rang. After a short conversation, it became obvious that duty would drag him away from one of his favourite pastimes.

Anthony's parents called to invite him out for dinner. He agreed to join them at the restaurant of their choice, because he was their only son; because he saw this as an opportunity to rejoice in the presence of loved ones; because it was important to maintain close family ties in these trying times; because he was hungry and needed a free meal.

Tossing aside his pies, Anthony prepared himself for an evening of fine dining. He searched through his closet for suitable attire. He went through several dinner jackets before finding the perfect one for his needs. He chose to wear his kangaroo hide jacket - aptly named, since kangaroos wear them as camouflage to hide in the bushes. He found a pair of black dress shoes. He found a black leather belt and a black tie. He found the Wilson's grandfather, who was reported missing four months ago. He thought about phoning Mr. and Mrs. Wilson about it, but they were in there as well. He found it strange that all three of them hadn't been reported missing.

Ignoring the Wilson family, Anthony found the perfect pair of dress trousers. He just bought them last week. They were fashioned out of recycled postage stamps. Not only were they environmentally-friendly, but also the envy of stamp collectors and postal officials alike.

Anthony slipped into his trousers, slowly and carefully. He was afraid the adhesiveness of the stamps might remove hair from his legs. He took great pride in his new trousers. Until now, he never had an occasion to wear them, or maybe this was just one of the few times he'd remembered to wear trousers at all. Regardless, he was soon ready and his parents were at his door.

Anthony's mother never looked more ravishing. She was wearing her favourite pair of army boots, which proved to be a perfect complement to her black pig-skin Victorian dress with a fluorescent-green ant painted on the front. Anthony's father was completely naked. Once again, he was going for the 'natural look' which no article of clothing seemed able to provide him with.

The Zen family was soon on the road, in search of a good restaurant. On the insistence of Anthony's mother, their first stop was 'The Pink Squid', a restaurant which specialized in pork schnitzel. The establishment was Mrs. Zen's preferred choice; because anyone wearing a fluorescent-green ant could enjoy all the pork schnitzel they could eat. It became obvious, considering her attire, that her heart was set on The Pink Squid from the get-go. You couldn't blame her; she could really pack away the pork schnitzel! However, her plan was ruined on account of her spouse. The 'no shirt, no shoes, no trousers, no money, no service' sign above the door seemed to suggest that Mr. Zen wouldn't be served. But at least he had money!

Returning to their quest for that perfect dining experience, Anthony's father suggested 'Yukon Fried Moose'. His reasoning was all too obvious. Anyone not wearing clothing could enjoy having a waitress sit on their lap while they ate. However, no sooner had the Zen family seated themselves than the owner of the restaurant raced out of the kitchen.

The owner, who was of obvious Viking descent, seemed highly agitated. He kept blinking and rubbing his eyes, as he wove through the packed restaurant, heading straight for the Zen's table. Stopping in front of their table, he was so dizzy he almost fell over. Before Anthony could ask him what was wrong, he demanded they all leave the restaurant. The owner claimed that after staring for several minutes at the fluorescent-green ant on Mrs. Zen's dress, he kept seeing bright green blotches every time he closed his eyes. Under the circumstances, the Zen family had no choice but to leave.

Having been turned away from two restaurants, the trio's hopes for an enjoyable evening of fine dining seemed dashed. Just when they were about to give up, go home and eat pies, Anthony spotted the solution. 'The Brass Sheep Leg' was a relatively new restaurant that specialized in seafood. Anthony figured that being

41

a new restaurant, the management was probably desperate enough for business that they'd let the Zen family in. He hoped they might even get to order some food.

Shortly after entering the restaurant, tragedy struck. It was inevitable. The dress code required that all gentlemen be wearing a tie. Of course, Anthony had his favourite black tie on, but what about his father? Anthony gave up without a word. He had just turned to head back to the car when he came upon a startling revelation. His father actually *was* wearing a tie - he had been all along!

Mr. Zen was wearing the tie Anthony bought him last Christmas. But it was no regular tie; it was the official Elvis Presley Memorial Tie. The tie was representative of the finest in quality craftsmanship. It displayed an immaculately embroidered picture of The King himself, along with the lyrics to all his songs - carefully stitched along the edges - and a scale drawing of the Presley Mansion, etched in silver. The tie also had the standard wooden carving of Elvis's guitar and several stills from his illustrious film career.

As you can imagine, it was a really big tie. Anthony was surprised he hadn't noticed his father wearing it until now. He figured he overlooked such a detail since it is not uncommon for an easily embarrassed son to ignore his virtually naked father in a restaurant environment.

Regardless, Anthony felt relieved. The tie was actually long enough to cover his father's private parts; in fact, the tie was long enough that it swept the floor clean as he dragged it along. Yet, the tie wasn't nearly as big as the official Donald Trump Tie Anthony gave his father for his last birthday. That particular tie consisted of two external hard drives connected to three personal computers. The computers, in turn, were connected to five separate data entry keyboards, six routers and twelve printers. Somewhere, amongst all the wires, was a telephone, an answering machine and two fax machines. The sole purpose of the tie was to count money. Unfortunately, Mr. Zen couldn't wear the tie, because it dislocated his left shoulder and nearly choked him to death. He gave the tie to a local charity, with the hopes that some poor, penniless soul might make use of it.

Anthony's attention was drawn away from the wonderful

world of ties - which rhymes with pies, oddly enough - when a waiter approached them. The waiter led the trio to their designated table. He politely asked them to take their seats.

"No thanks," Mr. Zen suddenly roared, "We have some at home!"

Ten minutes later, Mr. Zen was still laughing, but no one else in the restaurant got the joke. If people didn't notice his nakedness, he'd make a spectacle out of himself otherwise. Anthony got the impression that his father purposely forgot to wear his clothing just to get attention. However, Mrs. Zen assured Anthony that his father never wore clothing simply because he was incredibly stupid. A harsh indictment, Anthony thought to himself. Maybe his father deserved some credit; perhaps he was rebelling against a superficial clothing industry that turns citizens into walking billboards, encouraging the unsustainable consumption of cheaply produced garments sold at inflated prices. Maybe he was casting off labels and embracing the bare essentials - literally. Purging himself of distractions and getting to the essence of life. Running free with the animals, as nature intended. Mr. Zen took his napkin and began rubbing the embroidered Elvis on his tie. As he polished Elvis's face, the resulting reflection of light became so intense that Anthony had to squint to read the menu in front of him. On second thought, maybe his mother was on to something.

Mr. Zen almost wore himself out with his Elvis polishing. By that point, the tie emitted a brilliance that illuminated the entire restaurant. The management became worried. They liked to keep the restaurant dark, so the customers wouldn't notice that their seafood had been substituted with Bitesize Shredded Wheat.

Anthony's mother had always told him not to sit too close to a likeness of Elvis, because it was bad for his eyes. Heeding her advice, Anthony moved his chair as far away from his father's tie as possible, without having to leave the table altogether. Suddenly, Anthony was distracted by something completely different. He was about to discover why the restaurant was called 'The Brass Sheep Leg'.

It was barely audible at first, coming from the far side of the restaurant, nearly drowned out by the sounds of busy conversation and noisy eating. Anthony looked for the source of the sound, but he could find no explanation. Whatever it was, it seemed to be approaching their table, ever so slowly. Anthony guessed it was a three-legged man walking with a heavy metal cane. Yet, whatever it was, it was small enough that he couldn't see it approaching through the crowd. When the source of the curious sound finally came into view, Anthony was shocked at how close his guess really was.

The entire Zen family took notice of its presence. Mr. Zen was so stunned he temporarily put his Elvis polishing on hold. There, standing proudly in front of them, was a sheep with one brass leg.

The sheep owned the restaurant. He had lost a leg during the Great Australian Wool War of 1945. Luckily, his lost limb was replaced by a brass prosthetic which members of his flock constructed out of an old French horn.

"Excuse me, sir," the sheep began to address Mr. Zen politely, yet firmly, "I'm afraid you'll have to be seated elsewhere, due to the nature of your tie and the effect you are having on those around you."

Before Anthony's father could defend his actions, two waiters plucked him out of his chair. They carried him across the restaurant, his tie dragging along behind, until they reached a large, opaque glass box - pushed into a darkened corner. The waiters opened the box, tossed him in and closed the lid. Before returning to their regular duties, they made sure he had enough air.

"I hate Elvis," the sheep suddenly hollered, so that Mr. Zen could hear him from within his box. "He wore wool socks!"

Only Anthony's father could go into a restaurant and get scolded by a sheep.

"Excuse me," Anthony couldn't help but ask, "Where did you learn to speak English so well?"

"I had to learn English," the sheep replied, with some bitterness, "so that I could go undercover and breakup a POW camp where sheep were being mercilessly sheared."

The sheep hobbled back to the kitchen, stopping only to eat some salad that had fallen onto the floor. Anthony was left pondering why The Great Australian Wool War was never taught to him in school - probably because there weren't enough sheep enrolled to raise a fuss over it.

Anthony checked his watch; it was 9:00 a.m., but his

stomach thought it was much later than that. He was so hungry he could eat any animal large enough to ride on. His mother suggested they stop wasting time and order. They signalled for a waiter, while his poor father sat alone, completely secluded, in the opaque box that contained the radiance of his Elvis Presley Memorial Tie.

Anthony's mother just started some light, pre-dinner conversation when he realized, much to his horror, that they were seated directly across from two amphibian-like alien beings. Apparently, the aliens were sitting there for quite some time, quietly arguing over which was best: the original 'Star Trek' or 'Star Trek: the Next Generation'. Anthony couldn't help but take notice of them. One of the aliens made himself quite conspicuous when he leaped up from his chair and, clenching a handful of chips, raised his fist high above his head.

"Zonga!" he cried abruptly.

It was a simple one-word exclamation, to the ears of an Earthling. However, when translated from amphibious alien language, it takes on a slightly different meaning:

"These chips hold the secrets of the universe," he said, in actuality. "And they are mine alone! Not yours - all mine! I alone have the power, the glory, the saturated fats and high cholesterol level. My fries are tastier than yours - more golden brown than yours! They are fried to perfection!"

The other alien leaped up from his chair. Seizing a handful of jacket potatoes from his plate, he clutched his prize high above his head.

"Agnoz!" he retorted, which translates as follows:

"You are evil! But these jacket potatoes will protect me from your chips! My jacket potatoes are made from farm-fresh potatoes - not cut and frozen like yours! My potatoes have a rich potato flavour that just can't be beat. And even if you do defeat me, I will only become ten times stronger. May the force be with me!"

The entire restaurant watched in amazement, as bolts of energy streaked out of the potatoes that each alien clutched. The battle became so fierce and unrelenting that its rage illuminated every corner of the restaurant. Several customers suddenly realized - much to their dismay - that their Bitesize Shredded

Wheat, which had originally replaced their seafood, had been substituted with pitted prunes.

"If those two don't soon settle down and behave themselves," Anthony thought aloud, "then management might put *them* in an opaque box!"

As the aliens continued to fire their handfuls of chips and jacket potatoes at each other, the restaurant shook with a thunderous crackle of energy. It was actually one of the few times Anthony had been to a restaurant and not been able to hear the annoying cries of someone's baby; he was thankful for that. The battle became so intense that billows of steam rose up from the floor. Anthony panicked. He tried to save himself from embarrassment, but there was little he could do. He was a victim of circumstance. The rising steam penetrated his recycled postage stamp trousers, causing them to peel off. Anthony was trouserless once again. If he was going to write an autobiography, he'd call it "Forever Trouserless".

It seemed as though the two aliens would never stop their astronomical battle. Their hatred of each other's potatoes was just too strong. They had a complete disregard for the other customers, still trying to enjoy their meals amidst the bursting energy bolts, rising steam and thunderous quakes; some of them were having trouble signalling the waiter for their bill. Suddenly, the conflict ceased as a miraculous event unfolded. Anthony's mother was finally served her plate of boiled carrots.

The aliens were immediately agitated by the carrots. The alien brandishing the chips held them against his head.

"Gazon!" he whimpered, which translates as:

"Alas, behold a chip that is orange in colour, smooth in shape and soft in texture. It is more powerful than my chips. It holds the secrets of the universe, the power, the glory, the vitamin C that's good for your eyes. My power is meaningless. I am Mc Donald's chips. I am nothing."

There was a brief flash of light, followed by a plume of smoke. Using his handful of chips, the disgruntled alien blew his own head off. The other alien let his jacket potatoes fall to his plate. He motioned for the waiter.

"Ug," he grunted, which translates as:

"Could I have the bill, please?"

Anthony Goes to the Doctor

Anthony Zen awoke to the irritating electronic buzzing sound generated by his digital alarm clock. Sitting up in bed, he wiped the sleep from his eyes. He took a moment to remove a strand of hair from his mouth, hoping it was his own, as the alarm continued buzzing. Throwing back the covers, he was both pleased and surprised to discover a tuna casserole he'd been searching for since last week. Although the daredevil in him was tempted to sample the casserole, he chose instead to turn off his annoying alarm clock, before its high-pitched electronic whine drove him mad.

Stretching out towards the digital display, he tried pressing the 'off' button. He touched something warm and furry. With lightning reflexes, he withdrew his hand, tumbling off the bed. His reaction was due to a simple, sudden realisation: he didn't have a digital alarm clock. Wiping his eyes once again, since he didn't do a thorough job the first time, he peered up over the edge of the bed.

As usual, Anthony's cat was sitting on the dresser beside the bed. He was accustomed to Monty's annoying ringing. Every morning, he was plucked from the world of dreams by Monty's desperate bid for attention. Every morning, Monty sat motionless and watched Anthony's life slowly unfold. However, things had escalated; Anthony's beloved pet had somehow acquired the ability to project a digital display of the time from some sort of bio-luminescence within his stomach. He didn't have time to examine his demonic cat; according to the cat, it was 8:59 a.m., which meant he'd have to rush to make his 9:00 doctor's appointment.

Racing along the city streets, Anthony noticed several morning newspaper vendors. Among the most successful vendors were the Time Lords who sold newspapers from next week. However, the local pet grooming services wished to crack down on the Time Lords. It seemed that people were purchasing the newspapers, scanning the advertisements and flocking in with their pets to use coupons that claimed fifty percent off a clip and shampoo until the end of that particular week. What infuriated the pet groomers was the fact that pet owners were actually getting an entire extra week to take advantage of the fifty percent off deal. The whole problem was a confusing one.

Continuing to run along, Anthony became increasingly hot and uncomfortable. He could not understand why. Other passers-by seemed content and the weather was quite mild. Suddenly, fine American actor Kevin Kline leaped out of a restaurant and began making obscene gestures at him, while shouting rude comments about diminishing libido and demanding 'his cut'. Running past the raving madman, Anthony caught the tail end of his verbal assault.

"... and your line of underwear sucks!" he cried.

Only then did Anthony realize he'd forgotten to change out of his heavy wool pyjamas with a likeness of Kevin Kline on the front. His mother had knitted them for him, after a simple misunderstanding. Anthony had requested Calvin Klein pyjamas for Christmas. His mother, bless her heart, thought he said 'Kevin Kline' and set about knitting him what is perhaps the world's only pair of 'Kevin Kline Designer Pyjamas'. As mother would say: 'A homemade gift means so much more than something purchased." But try explaining that to Kevin Kline!

Shortly afterwards, Anthony arrived at the doctor's office. He approached the receptionist.

"My name is Anthony Zen," he announced proudly, "and I have come for my appointment with Dr. Kilimanjaro."

The receptionist did not respond. An elderly woman, she wore a pair of bottle-bottom nerd glasses, except she forgot to remove the fizzy drink from the bottles. Anthony figured she didn't see him come in.

"I'm here now," he hollered, leaning in so close to her that he could see his reflection swimming in her glasses. "I'm here for my appointment."

The receptionist remained silent. Thinking she was deaf, and rather blind, Anthony reached over and patted her on the head - an optimistic attempt at getting her attention. The receptionist responded by collapsing over her desk. Her bottle-bottom glasses broke on impact and a puddle of effervescing cola quickly formed. Only then did he notice the intravenous attached to her arm. She wasn't a receptionist after all, but a patient. He thought it would be best to just leave her alone. He went over to the waiting room chairs and sifted through the magazines.

Anthony loved to read waiting room magazines at both the

doctor's office and the dentist's office (it didn't really matter which, since they usually traded magazines). He was amazed at how much useful information a person could gain through a few wisely spent minutes in the waiting room. Checking his watch, he was pleased to see it was 9:00 a.m. Any minute now, he would be ushered in for his appointment. Meanwhile, however, he had lots of time to read.

Anthony found an old issue of 'Cosmopolitan' with articles on how to do your hair, how to crack an egg, how to get dressed and how to make love to a man. Underneath that was an issue of 'International Coffee Pot' which contained a pictorial history of the modern coffee pot. Then there was another issue of 'Cosmopolitan', containing articles on how to get dressed, how to make toast, how to do your hair and how to make love to a man.

Beneath a copy of 'A Doctor's Guide to Scabs and Open Sores' was an issue of 'Trout and Salmon Magazine', featuring an article on how to maximise beer can litter along stream banks. Also on hand was an issue of 'The Book of Dankles'. Anthony had never heard of a 'dankle' before. After browsing through the publication, he got the impression that no one else had heard of them either.

Moving deeper into the magazine pile, Anthony found yet another issue of 'Cosmopolitan' with articles on how to get dressed, how to make maple syrup, how to do your hair and how to make love to a man. He paused to reflect on the quality of information contained in 'Cosmopolitan'. He thought how wonderful it would be if all women read it. The result would be a superior race of well-dressed women with beautiful hair who could make love with surgical precision and make great eggs, toast and maple syrup to boot! What more could a man ask for? Anthony himself would be the first one to admit to loving breakfast items.

Beneath a pile of confidential patient files, Anthony found an issue of 'Reader's Digest'. It featured a story about a young man with an ear ache who goes to the doctor's office only to waste most of his time reading magazines.

"What rubbish!" Anthony shrieked, so that anyone who happened to be listening might share his contempt.

Anthony gave the issue of 'Reader's Digest' to the elderly lady seated next to him. She didn't thank him. She had been sitting in the waiting room since last week; now she was quite dead. Ignoring the elderly lady, since she ignored him first, he continued to sift through the magazine pile. He uncovered an issue of the official 'W.W.E. Magazine'. Flipping through the magazine, he found articles on body slams, headlocks, big fat bellies, tag team wrestling, grilled cheese sandwiches, pile-drivers and - oddly enough - an article on how to make love to a man.

Anthony's reading was interrupted by the appearance of a respectable-looking gentleman.

"Anthony Zen?" the man called out.

"Yes," Anthony responded, happy that his wait was over.

"We're ready for you now."

Anthony set down his magazine and approached the entrance of the examining room. The man stood there waiting.

"You don't look like a doctor," Anthony frowned, drawing closer. "I'm supposed to be seeing Doctor Kilimanjaro."

"I know that," the man replied dryly. "I am Doctor Kilimanjaro's psychiatrist."

"Oh," Anthony nodded, not knowing what else to say.

"Anthony," the psychiatrist placed his arm around Anthony, as if he needed his trust, "I'm afraid I need a favour from you."

"Why's that?" Anthony looked towards the examination room. "Is something wrong?"

"Yes, there is something wrong, Anthony," the psychiatrist nodded. "Doctor Kilimanjaro has been under my care for quite some time now. He seems to be reliving a devastating series of events that occurred when he was a member of the Swiss Navy - in fact, he was the only member. I think he has mountain madness. Even worse, when he was vacationing in the jungles of Central America, after completing a top secret mission for the Icelandic Secret Service, he became involved in a terrible cannibalism scandal. I think you can see what all this means, Anthony," he paused, tapping Anthony on the head, just to make sure he was still awake. "Doctor Kilimanjaro has developed a strong aversion to shiny metallic objects."

"Maybe I should come back some other day," Anthony perked up, having been tapped on the head.

"That wouldn't be a good idea," the psychiatrist stopped Anthony from leaving. "It would be in my patient's best interest if you let him examine you. He hasn't had a patient in over three years. If you see him, it would help with his therapy. His present psychological state might improve significantly. Don't worry," the psychiatrist pushed Anthony into the examining room, "just think of the great service you'll be performing for Doctor Kilimanjaro."

The psychiatrist seated Anthony in the examination chair.

"I'll be observing from over here," he said, taking out a pen and notebook and seating himself on the far side of the room.

Anthony looked around the room. He couldn't see the doctor anywhere. He wondered if mountain madness had caused the doctor to want to hide on his patients. He began to feel uneasy. The psychiatrist's presence didn't help. He busied himself writing in his notebook, leaving Anthony feeling completely alone. A tree limb rubbed against the window. Anthony jumped. The psychiatrist looked up from his notebook. Anthony felt silly - scared of the wind. But suddenly the window flew open. A gust of wind and leaves flew into the room, closely followed by Doctor Kilimanjaro.

Anthony was shocked, to say the least, by the doctor's theatrical entrance. However, more than anything, he was shocked by the doctor's appearance.

"What ... what ...," Doctor Kilimanjaro stammered, in a trance-like state, "what is your problem?"

"Well," Anthony replied nervously, his body rigid, "I've got an ear ache."

"I look in ear!" the doctor shouted, from beneath his enormous owl mask.

While Doctor Kilimanjaro leaped away to find an instrument, Anthony thought about what caught him off guard the most: the doctor's elaborate mask, or the string of shrunken heads around his neck. The doctor returned with a small metallic flashlight. However, just as he was about to examine Anthony's ear, he became transfixed. Clutching the instrument before him, he shook so violently that some ostrich feathers fell from his mask.

"Shiny! Shiny!" he screamed, stomping his bare feet on the floor.

The psychiatrist rushed over and forced him to drop the flashlight.

"Think jujubes," the psychiatrist pleaded, wrestling with his patient, "think liquorice flavoured jujubes!"

Surprisingly enough, the doctor calmed down while panting 'jujubes, jujubes' over and over again. The psychiatrist turned to Anthony.

"A close call," he winked, smiled, suddenly became quite serious, tidied his suit jacket and returned to his seat to jot down a few notes.

Anthony didn't know what to think. He thought about starting a stamp collection, but before he could plan all the details, Doctor Kilimanjaro was ready to attend to him again.

"Open wide," the doctor grunted, holding a tongue depressor. "Tongue depressor is wood. Is good - not shiny!"

While the doctor examined his throat, Anthony reminded him about his ear ache. Anthony became quite worried when he was asked to slip out of his trousers. Perhaps he was most concerned about the fact that he wasn't wearing any trousers to begin with. Apparently, the doctor couldn't see out of his owl mask very well and didn't realize Anthony was wearing only pyjama tops and boxer shorts.

It took some convincing, but Anthony finally got the doctor to examine his ear. He looked at Anthony's left ear and shook his head, as if something was wrong. He proceeded to the right ear. After a brief examination, he paused and scratched his stomach in wonderment. He scratched Anthony's stomach as well. Anthony was anxious to know the diagnosis.

"You have only two ears?" the doctor asked. "Yes," Anthony answered, "as far as I know."

"That's a good sign!" the doctor announced.

Doctor Kilimanjaro stepped back, staring at Anthony through the narrow holes in his elaborate owl mask.

"I take blood pressure now," he informed Anthony. "An apple a day leaves you with an empty bushel by the end of the year."

Anthony expected the worst, as the doctor headed towards a cabinet full of shiny metallic objects to fetch a blood pressure monitor. Disaster was imminent. Anthony looked towards the psychiatrist, to see what he intended to do. But he was too preoccupied with the ink blotch on his collar which he thought looked like a spider - or a butterfly, or a flower, or Sigmund Freud's facial hair.

Doctor Kilimanjaro flung open the cabinet and seized the shiny instruments. He began to howl like a Swiss yodeller closing the refrigerator door on a coyote's tail. He danced around the room, flinging the instruments into the air. His hips moved in a circular fashion, emphasizing the hula skirt Anthony just noticed him wearing. Trying to avoid the rain of shiny metallic objects, the psychiatrist rushed forth.

"Think jujubes! Think liquorice jujubes!" he cried, leaping onto the doctor's back.

Doctor Kilimanjaro didn't seem to be responding to his therapy. With the psychiatrist on his back, he ran round and round the examination chair which Anthony was too afraid to get up from.

"Think jujubes! Think liquorice jujubes!" the psychiatrist pleaded with him.

However, his demands were barely audible. He kept pausing to sneeze - apparently allergic to the ostrich feathers on the doctor's owl mask - and the doctor, beating on his chest, began to sing the theme from the Spiderman cartoons.

Doctor Kilimanjaro eventually wore himself out. Most doctors do tend to lead stressful lifestyles. With the psychiatrist still on his back, he collapsed to the ground, just as he completed the last line of the song:

"Wherever there's a hang-up, you'll find the Spiderman!" he groaned.

The psychiatrist turned Doctor Kilimanjaro over, removed his elaborate owl mask, sneezed three times and tried to coax his patient into eating a handful of liquorice jujubes. Anthony, sensing that his appointment was over, got up from the examination chair and tip-toed towards the door. Leaving the examination room, he thought he heard the psychiatrist call out to him, thanking him for his patience and support, or maybe he was just sneezing; Anthony's ear was still aching too much to tell for sure. Regardless, Anthony left the building and headed for home.

All Cats are Grey

It was a simply gorgeous day. Cancer-causing solar radiation blazed down through cloudless skies. People everywhere tore off their clothing, exposing copious pale flesh that should never see the light of day. Blinded by their folly, desperate for vitamin D, like lemmings drawn to the cliffs, they offered themselves to a Sun God who showed no mercy on their lilywhite hides. Sunburns, heat stroke and blurred vision were all the rage. People rushed to partake. No sooner had one poor soul been carted off – either 'well done' or 'overcooked' – then another rushed in to take his place. Children screamed above the constant din of honking horns, because their ice-cream had melted. Families trapped in cars, without air conditioning, begged passersby for a sip of water – women and children first! The very fabric of society was coming apart at the seams. You could cook an egg on the pavement, if you had an egg and the time – or a chicken and the patience. A Chicken – good luck catching him on a day like today! He crossed the road. Why did the chicken cross the road? Well, that's another story! Suffice to say, it was a perfect day for Anthony Zen and his friend Jemmy to casually stroll the city streets in search of a good argument. It did not take long for the basis of a good argument to enter Anthony's head, via his right ear.

"Vegetarianism is a bad idea," Anthony began, knowing Jemmy would surely retaliate with a heated counter attack. "People must eat beef. If we don't, the cow population will get out of control and wild cows will roam the countryside, devouring our children."

Jemmy remained silent. He seemed to be carefully considering how to argue against Anthony's statement. Seizing the opportunity, Anthony continued to support his case.

"Have you ever noticed that cows don't look at you when you honk your horn at them?" he watched Jemmy, carefully monitoring his reaction. "That's not due to simple ignorance. They're silently plotting to overthrow the human race! We must eat them all!"

"You're right," Jemmy nodded, "vegetarianism is a bad idea."

Anthony was shocked that Jemmy gave up so easily.

Actually, he was somewhat angry with Jemmy; a proper argument was not in the works after all.

"I thought you told me you were a vegetarian," Anthony ventured, trying to discover why Jemmy chose not to argue.

"I'm a vegetarian only in the sense that I eat animals that eat vegetables," Jemmy explained.

During the next few hours, strolling around the city streets, Anthony was equally unsuccessful in creating a proper argument. Jemmy seemed more interested in seeing how much attention he could attract with his flamboyant Viking outfit, which he always wore; he put very little effort into forming a solid argument. However, Jemmy was not attracting that much attention. All the pedestrian traffic seemed distracted by a troubled, badly burnt sunbather running wildly around the streets, with a revolver in hand, screaming "Someone please kill me!" at the top of his lungs.

"Would not have happened if he brought the sunscreen - and left the gun at home," Jemmy opined, straining to see through the slits in his elaborate owl mask.

Anthony had no time to feel sympathy for the beet-red sun worshipper; he was dodging small meteorites that periodically fell from the cloudless skies above him. Anthony hated meteorite showers; an otherwise perfect day could be completely ruined by the gradual accumulation of intergalactic geological oddities in his tangled mop of hair. Luckily, Jemmy was able to remove all of the burning space rocks from Anthony's hair, before a bad case of split ends set in, using a pair of asbestos gloves he always carried for such emergencies.

Regardless of his meteorite dodging, and Jemmy's persistent banging on the ceremonial drum he always carried, Anthony became increasingly bored. However, the mundane atmosphere surrounding him was suddenly diffused when a truly astronomical observation struck him. He quickly developed his observation into a deeply scientific and philosophical theory - a theory which would not only spark a feverish debate between Jemmy and himself, but would surely have resounding effects, becoming a topic of heated discussion for generations to come.

When Anthony was ready to share his brilliant theory with the rest of the world, he gathered his wits and shouted aloud with a prestigious, confident voice:

"ALL CATS ARE GREY!!"

"No they're not," Jemmy retorted.

"Yes, they are!"

"Are not!"

"Yes."

"No."

Anthony had a feeling his theory had begun an intense - and undoubtedly successful - argument. Yet it was in its early stages and he didn't want to seem too presumptuous. He waited with eager anticipation for Jemmy to thoroughly cross examine his theory, so he could defend it with full confidence. His opportunity presented itself after Jemmy took a few minutes to think about the problem.

"Ah-hah!" Jemmy raised a finger, speaking with an air of wisdom. "All cats are not grey, because there are also black ones!"

"True, but black is just one of the colours that comprises the colour grey," Anthony explained. "Therefore, a black cat can easily be classified as grey, because they are so closely related."

Anthony tried to conceal his excitement; it seemed Jemmy was at a complete loss to find anything wrong with his theory. However, Jemmy would not give up so easily.

"But what about white cats?" he asked.

Anthony laughed out loud; he had planned for such an obstacle to his theory.

"Well, white cats are easy to explain," he started. "You see, white is nothing more than a colour that combines with black to form grey. Therefore, I can conclude that all black cats, and all white cats, are derived from an ancestral grey cat which is clearly genetically dominant to all others. Thus, it is safe to say that all cats are, in fact, grey!"

Jemmy rubbed his chin – or at least it seemed he was rubbing his chin, beneath his owl mask. Then he rubbed Anthony's chin. Was he completely convinced? Anthony could feel victory coming to visit him. He envisioned the lifestyle of a scholar. Soon, he too would be gathering in the study; reclining in a velvet chair beside the fireplace, puffing his pipe; checking the pockets of his smoking jacket for more tobacco, or perhaps a revised theory of relativity he scratched down during breakfast. Yes, this was his destiny, now that he had an iron-clad theory. His thoughts were interrupted when Jemmy stopped rubbing his chin (Anthony's, that is) and snapped his fingers.

"What about ginger cats?" Jemmy smiled curiously.

Anthony felt his stomach drop. Blood rushed to his head, his ears rang and his ankles ached. He could not think of a way to explain ginger coloured cats within the context of his theory. It appeared as though victory had called and cancelled its visit. He had no choice but to admit defeat in front of Jemmy. However, in this darkest of hours, he was suddenly saved from admitting defeat by a rather unusual event.

Although the meteorite shower had subsided, an unusually large meteorite suddenly crashed to the ground, just a short distance away from Anthony and Jemmy. The result of the spectacular impact was a chain of catastrophic events including: buildings collapsing, flames shooting into the air, cars exploding and people biting into fruit that had not been washed.

"Holy cow! Did you see that meteorite land?" Anthony screamed, with a mixed tone of fear and excitement.

"Don't change the subject!" Jemmy persisted, above all the racket. "What about ginger cats?"

Just then, a massive cloud of fluorescent gas rose upwards from the hole created by the enormous meteorite. It was followed by the appearance of the oddest abomination Anthony had ever laid eyes on. His lower jaw dropped just enough for a dentist to recommend a check-up from the other side of the street. It was almost too incredible, but it was not an illusion brought on by the afternoon heat; his senses were too alert to be fooled. Hovering before him, he knew it was foreign to his plane of existence. It was nothing more than a fleshy sphere covered with thousands of small ears.

"Are you seeing what I'm seeing?" Anthony tugged on Jemmy. "How can this be happening to us? What does it want and where is it from?"

"Who cares?" Jemmy pulled away. "What about the ginger cats, Mr. Know-It-All?"

It struck Anthony that the unusual sphere of alien flesh and thousands of ears, still hovering in front of him, was probably an infinitely intelligent, all-knowing being from some far superior planet. So he decided to confront the alien life form with his perplexing theory.

"Oh great and wonderful alien entity," he began politely.

"Can a mere mortal, such as me, trouble you with a question which is of utmost importance?"

"I'm all ears," the alien replied.

"Are all cats grey?"

"No fair!" Jemmy interjected. "You can't ask him - that's cheating!"

"Yes," the alien replied, ignoring Jemmy's comment, "it is true that all cats are grey."

"Told you so!" Anthony laughed, Jemmy becoming quite upset.

"All right then," Jemmy crossed his arms, nodding at the alien sphere of a thousand ears, "what about ginger cats?"

"Ginger cats are evil," the alien life form began, still hovering before them. "They are a genetic abnormality - a mutation which must be destroyed before they spread like cancer and wipe out all of the proper cats. That is why I came to Earth - to destroy all of the ginger cats! My many ears will lead me to them. First, I must take control of the airwaves. I will rally grey cats together through a vast communications network. To assist me, I will use your Earth methods – what you call, 'popular song'. I have written a song called 'All Cats are Grey'. And now I must begin my mission. Grey cats await me. Ginger cats fear me. Thank you for your question, little human - and clean your ears regularly!"

"What about brown cats - and Siamese?" Jemmy stamped his feet, causing feathers to fall from his owl mask.

The alien sphere of a thousand ears disappeared in the blink of an eye.

"It didn't even answer me," Jemmy shook his head, feeling disappointed. "In one ear and out the other, I guess."

With the alien sphere gone from sight, Anthony and Jemmy continued their walk along the city streets. Although they kept searching for a new topic of discussion, nothing came up to relieve the boredom of their late afternoon walk.

Grandma was a Ninja

Anthony Zen drove another spike into the mountain's rocky face. He carefully attached another length of rope, as a safe guard against his falling back down the two thousand feet he had just scaled. With the rope securely in place, he resumed his ascent into the heavens.

Anthony was but one man against the barren, snow-swept peaks of the most notorious mountain in the universe. He realized long ago that it only took one wrong move, one poorly placed foot, to send him hurtling down the mountain's icy face to greet certain death far below. But it was too late for him to turn back now; his efforts would not be in vain. Climbing slowly and carefully, he skilfully chose each hand-hold and footing on the near perpendicular slope of the mighty Mount Tingtension.

Anthony thought only of his final goal, as the unrelenting wind and snow tried to pry him from the cliff face. Only through the power of positive thinking, combined with careful respect for the very elements he was battling, could he reach Mount Tingtension's tallest and most elusive peak.

Anthony exercised an exceptionally great deal of caution when approaching the Boy Scout troop. Clinging onto a single rope - huddled together for protection against the cold, harsh mountain climate - they presented somewhat of an obstacle to his climb. However, he soon found that their belts made for safe, convenient hand-holds; their shoulders - though young and weak - made for acceptable footing.

As Anthony climbed over the Boy Scouts, they asked him if he would like to buy a box of cookies. He declined the offer; cookies were bad for his teeth. Rotting teeth were a problem he could definitely do without. All his concentration had to be placed on his ascent. He had no time to be brushing his teeth. Mount Tingtension was a notoriously dangerous mountain; its fury could easily consume any young man who paid too much attention to dental hygiene while climbing.

Anthony decided to take a brief rest, to regain his strength. Peering down at the suspended Boy Scout troop, now some twenty feet below, he pondered the history and geography of the majestic mountain.

Mount Tingtension was located along the rocky coast of central Holland. Geologists, seismologists and people who are just fond of rocks claim that the Mount Tingtension range originates in Holland; where it then twists through Belgium, passes through Germany, cuts up through Russia, bends back to France, completely avoids Switzerland and continues to China where it goes beneath the earth and resurfaces somewhere in the Canadian Prairies.

Mount Tingtension had gained a foreboding reputation, because of the long history of fatal accidents on its steep, treacherous slopes. Climbers often fell, froze to death, or got tangled in their ropes. The last recorded accident involved an experienced Swiss climber who had just opened a brand new pair of finely crafted leather mountain climbing boots. As the rest of his expedition looked on in horror, he reached into the bottom of one boot and removed a small packet which read: 'Do Not Eat'. In a sudden burst of carelessness - uncharacteristic of experienced Swiss climbers - he accidentally swallowed the small packet. Needless to say, he was never heard from again.

Anthony quickly erased the frightening history of Mount Tingtension from his mind; otherwise, fear, apprehension and an intense craving for oven-baked fish cakes would prevent him from reaching his final goal - the uppermost peak.

It was on the uppermost, snow-covered peak that Anthony hoped to meet a legendary ancient wise man who was all-seeing, all-knowing and freezing cold as well. Some say the man wasn't mortal; he had been living there, in complete isolation, for eons. But regardless of what the others had told him, Anthony wanted to meet the man for himself. He wanted to experience the spiritual Xanadu that the wise man had diligently maintained across the eons – high above the noise, pollution and distractions of modern life.

Anthony felt a sudden burst of excitement, realizing he had finally reached the apex of the mountain. His hands grasped what seemed to be the sides of a completely flat surface atop the mountain. He pulled himself up onto level ground. Much to his delight, his eyes finally fell upon the ancient wise man. The wise man had a characteristically long silvery beard, flowing white robe, gnarled wooden walking stick, golden sandals and a book of carpet samples which he flipped through eagerly.

Anthony was surprised to see several men running about the mountain top carrying boards, windows and furniture. Diggers brought in loads of brick, cement trucks brought in mortar and small delivery trucks deposited ornamental shrubberies. The ancient wise man suddenly spoke up above all the racket caused by the machinery and labourers.

"Fuchsia! Fuchsia!" he cried in anger. "What the hell kind of colour is fuchsia?"

He tossed the book of carpet samples at a rather feminine looking interior decorator standing beside him.

"Why, it's a simply lovely colour!" the interior decorator explained. "It's a combination of a nice light pink colour and white …"

"ARRGH!!" the wise man stamped his feet. "If you had been living on a pile of snow for the last forty-two million years, do you think you'd want a 'nice light colour' carpet!!? Now, listen to me," his eyes grew larger, stabbing a wrinkled finger into the decorator's chest, "I want a big, bold carpet with lots of blue, green and huge slabs of black!! Understand?"

The interior decorator hustled away - speechless, but nodding in agreement. The wise man finally noticed Anthony's presence.

"What are you doing up here?" he asked.

"I carefully, and skilfully, climbed all the way up this treacherous mountain to see you - all great and knowing one," Anthony replied, proud of his accomplishment.

The wise man looked Anthony up and down. No doubt, he was impressed by Anthony's strength and perseverance. After all, Anthony's impressive array of mountain climbing equipment - all secured to his person - was testimonial to his dedication to climbing. The pieces of snow and ice lodged in his hair and brows were testimonial to the battle he fought to reach the top. And the baggy boxer shorts were testimonial to the fact he had forgotten to wear his trousers. The wise man looked Anthony in the face and paused for what seemed an eternity to Anthony, but a mere blink of an eye to the ancient wise man.

"Why didn't you just take the elevator?" the wise man shrugged.

"Elevator!" Anthony cried. "What elevator!"

"The one running through the centre of the mountain," the wise man motioned. "The elevator doors are located down where the bus route ends."

"Bus route!" Anthony shrieked, pieces of melting snow and ice falling from his hair, water running down his face. "What bus route?" he wiped his brow. "I hiked to the base of the mountain!"

A stunned look came across the wise man's face. He reached out and put his hand firmly on Anthony's shoulder. Anthony - standing there, tired and shaking - took this as a gesture of support and sympathy. But when the wise man fell against him and began to roar with uncontrollable laughter, he realised that the wise man only wanted to avoid falling to the ground.

The wise man experienced tear-filled convulsions of laughter for what seemed like the time required for a small black kitten to completely digest an entire turnip. But as far as the ancient wise man was concerned, it was merely the time required for a small black kitten to decide not to eat an entire turnip. Anthony, his face red with embarrassment, his feet green with unpleasant fungus, had to support the frail old wise man through the entire ordeal. The situation worsened when the wise man turned to the construction workers around him.

"Hey boys," he sobbed, between fits of laughter. "This guy hiked all the way to the base of the mountain. Then climbed all the way up!" he paused, laughing so hard that he nearly pulled Anthony to the ground. "He didn't even know there was an elevator!"

The entire work crew joined the wise man in a good laugh. Anthony felt about as embarrassed as any young man stuck on a mountain top without trousers, standing in front of several construction workers, with an eccentric old man hanging off of him. However, he had already been through enough. He definitely wasn't going to let this incident divert him from his true purpose. Standing as tall as he could, he ignored the laughter and announced his intentions.

"Oh great, magnificent, bearded, elderly wise man," he spoke out above the laughter, "I have many questions that I wish you to answer."

But before Anthony could continue, he heard a sharp scream. It sounded as though someone had fallen from the side of the mountain. The wise man, hearing the scream as well, quickly regained his composure. He followed Anthony, racing to the edge to see what had happened. Anthony peered over and saw that one member of the Boy Scout troop, suspended below, had lost his grip on the rope and was now plummeting out of sight.

The wise man stepped up to the edge, beside Anthony, and hollered down to the remaining Boy Scouts, dangling from the rope.

"Haven't you kids gone home yet?"

One of the Boy Scouts looked upwards towards the wise man.

"Do you have a telephone I could use?" he hollered back, hoping to be heard. "I would like to call my parents and let them know where I am."

"No, I don't have a telephone!" the wise man screeched. "What the hell do you think I'm running up here - a fish factory?" The ancient wise man turned to Anthony. "It used to be real nice and quiet up here, until I wanted to get this house built. Now these damn kids are bugging me all the time and I've just about ..."

The wise man was interrupted by the screams of another Boy Scout plummeting to his death.

"Are you sure you don't have a telephone?" hollered another Boy Scout, who was rubbing some twigs against the rock face in a desperate attempt at lighting a fire.

"I want to go home!" cried another, hanging on for dear life, shivering in the cold.

"Do you want to buy some cookies?" asked another.

"You stupid, snotty-nosed little bastards!" the wise man shook his fist. "You're supposed to be selling apples - not cookies! Cookies are for Girl Guides!"

"Where the hell are we supposed to find apples on a mountain in the middle of Holland?" retorted one of the Boy Scouts, just before losing his grip and rocketing downward.

"Kids these days - they'll argue about anything!" the wise man shook his head. He turned to Anthony. "Now, what can I help you with, young man?"

"I require your vast wisdom, infinite intellect and lucky guessing to answer three great questions which have troubled me as of late," Anthony replied, relieved that he was finally being serviced.

"Go ahead, ask away!" the wise man insisted, raising his arms upwards - perhaps to make himself look more important, but most likely to put his brand new antiperspirant to the test.

"Okay, here's my first question," Anthony paused. He straightened himself up and cleared his throat, to further prepare for his long awaited question. He had come this far. Now, beyond a doubt, he was ready. "Oh great and wise one," he began, feeling confident, "What is the meaning of life?"

"Easy," the wise man shrugged. "It's a series of completely random events dictated by simple chemical reactions. Next!"

"Oh great and wise one," Anthony began anew, for he was just warming up, "is Certs a breath mint, or is it merely a candy mint?"

"Ah," the wise man rubbed the long silvery hairs covering his chin, "that is a question which many young mountain climbers like yourself have ventured to ask me. Suffice it to say that while Certs is a breath mint to adults," he paused in thought, "it is a mere candy mint to children."

"Amazing!" Anthony cried.

"What's your final question?" the ancient wise man pressed on, wishing to avoid excessive praise for his intellectual capabilities.

"Well," Anthony crossed his arms. An even more challenging question suddenly came to mind, replacing all other thoughts, "Why is this story called 'Grandma was a Ninja'?"

"Anthony," the wise man sighed, shaking his head, "not even I know the answer to that!"

Shakespeare Unplugged

Anthony Zen kept himself extremely busy, feverishly rummaging through the old wooden trunk residing in his unkempt closet. His ecstatic rummaging was completely necessary. He was trying his best to find an old photo album, a pair of winter boots, an umbrella and his neighbour's Doberman pinscher.

After a long period of searching, Anthony still couldn't locate any of the aforementioned items. However, he did manage to inadvertently discover a musty collection of worm-eaten papers, which turned out to be the previously unavailable works of William Shakespeare. He was rather surprised with his rare find. But more importantly, he was relieved that his neighbour's Doberman pinscher wasn't in his wooden trunk! He was afraid the dog might bite him.

After eating supper, watching some television, weaving a few baskets, showering, playing a rigorous game of cricket and showering again, it suddenly struck Anthony that his discovery could change the way the world thinks about classical literature - not the discovery that his neighbour's Doberman pinscher wasn't in his trunk, but the other discovery: the rare Shakespearean plays.

Flipping through the ancient pile of papers, Anthony could barely read any of the writing. Everything was obviously written with pen and quill; it seemed to be merely rough work. Amongst the pages were scenes from a number of plays that Shakespeare chose to remove from his final drafts. In some cases, the entire outcome of a play would have been completely different. Surprisingly, there was also a collection of Shakespeare's Jewish jokes. Anthony chose to ignore the jokes. They were too offensive for his delicate sensibilities, although the one about the sausage was quite witty.

After some careful consideration, Anthony decided on the best way to present this extremely rare collection of Shakespeare's early works to a drama-starved public - he'd simply publish them all together, as one big compilation! He figured that working on the compilation would give him a break from his own literary endeavours. After all, he had recently come down with a bad case of writer's cramp - an ailment usually avoided if you remember to wait one hour, after writing a story, before going swimming.

Thus, through hard work, determination, a love for classical literature and a genuine need to clean the rubbish out of his closet and get as much cash for it as he could, Anthony compiled 'Shakespeare Unplugged'. When it was finally ready for publication, it read something like this …

"What's that you have there?" a voice broke the silence gathered just above Anthony's right shoulder.

Startled, Anthony turned from his manuscript and looked up. A trail of pipe smoke led to a pipe. The pipe led to two pursed lips. The lips, sheltered under an immaculate silver moustache, drew carefully on the pipe. The moustache shared real estate with an equally well-groomed silver beard. The beard was a good neighbour; straight and narrow and not a spot of soup in sight. The real estate was a solid, weathered piece of land with a few deep furrows but well maintained over all. Two pools of inquisitive blue were sunken into it, each shaded by lively silver brows. A thin stand of silver surrounded the land; hardly private, but a comfy resting place for the hat he favoured. The land was interrupted by an overpass - a pair of round-frame spectacles - but other than that it all appeared natural and untainted by everything except the passing years.

"It's my Shakespeare manuscript," Anthony pulled back, since his guest - hovering above his right shoulder - was too close for comfort. "I've found a bunch of his unproduced plays in my old wooden trunk."

"Really," the man puffed on his pipe, surveying Anthony's flat. "That's quite the story."

Anthony got a good look at his guest. He was wearing a tie that only men of a certain vintage could get away with. His cardigan was of possible historical significance. His slippers suggested he was always comfortable, regardless of time or place. His brown baggy trousers condemned him to a life of fashion crime.

"Excuse me," Anthony spoke up, distracting his guest from his surveying. "Who are you?"

"I'm a pompous critic," the man replied proudly. "I have a pipe and everything."

Anthony was taken aback. He had never met a pompous critic before. He didn't know what to say or do. He had no idea why the pompous critic was in his flat, or how he got there. He must have escaped from a university. At any rate, Anthony had to think fast.

Perhaps his every word would be scrutinized from this moment on.

"Really," Anthony replied, although his delayed response was met with a look of suspicion. "That's quite the story."

"Mmmm," the pompous critic puffed his pipe, looking Anthony in the eye. "Yes, it is quite a story, isn't it?"

The pompous critic pulled up a chair next to Anthony. The chair had heavy, dark wood legs and arms – immaculately carved. It was covered in rich burgundy leather. Anthony had never seen the chair before. The pompous critic must have brought it with him. One of the tools of the trade, Anthony figured.

"Now then," the pompous critic crossed his legs carefully, "let's have a look at this so-called Shakespearean manuscript of yours."

"What do you mean 'so-called'," Anthony countered, holding up the manuscript. "It's signed and dated by William himself."

"That may well be the case," the pompous critic smiled confidently, "but I've seen many fakes in my time – particularly in relation to William Shakespeare."

"Are you saying I've faked this?" Anthony shook the manuscript.

"Not necessarily," the pompous critic replied. "Perhaps it was faked by someone else."

"As I said, it's signed and dated," Anthony held some of the manuscript up as evidence. "And the papers look old – so does the writing."

"That appears to be the case," the pompous critic nodded slowly, pipe smoke swirling round him. "But these things are all easily faked."

"I assure you," Anthony pleaded, "I found them in my old wooden trunk."

"You honestly expect me to believe you were rummaging in an old wooden trunk trying to find an old photo album, a pair of winter boots, an umbrella and your neighbour's Doberman pinscher and instead you found a priceless collection of William Shakespeare's unpublished plays?"

"Yes," Anthony replied confidently, although he was uncertain how the pompous critic knew why he was rummaging in the first place.

"Well, to each his own," the pompous critic shrugged. He looked around the flat. He noted the collection of round objects lining the high shelves. Anthony's cat Monty, sleeping soundly in a corner, issued a guttural ringing sound with each breath. "But this all seems more unlikely by the moment."

"What seems unlikely?" Anthony looked about nervously.

"I supposed you're accustomed to this," the pompous critic began, "but to an outsider's eyes a rare Shakespeare manuscript discovered in this environment seems a bit of a stretch."

"There's only one way to settle this!" Anthony announced proudly.

"I agree," the pompous critic nodded. "Read it - read it and let's settle this once and for all."

Anthony, always willing to oblige, cleared his throat. He began reading his manuscript, exactly as he had planned it …

INTRODUCTION:

Imagine my surprise at finding rare, never-before-seen segments of Shakespeare's plays, diaries and letters. Or imagine a naked woman climbing down your chimney. Whichever you choose, the end result is sheer joy. And like a soot-covered woman emerging from a fireplace, interrupting a dinner party and asking to use the telephone, this collection is liable to create a stir.

Assuming that the collection is genuine, it demonstrates that even William Shakespeare was capable of writing something which was best kept hidden in a closet. Judging by some of his frilly clothing, maybe he kept himself hidden in a closet as well. But who am I to judge a master? I don't pretend to be an authority on Shakespeare or his life. With this in mind, I leave it up to you, humble reader, to draw your own conclusions regarding Shakespeare's artistic merit. And that is why I present to you 'Shakespeare Unplugged'.

Anthony Zen

"Still with me?" Anthony paused.

"An adequate introduction," the pompous critic nodded. "You've managed to capture my attention – you may continue."

This first selection appears to be an alternate ending for the original draft of the now classic 'King Lear'. But for some strange reason, it was abandoned.

SCENE IV: Enter Lear, Oswald and the Janitor

Lear: Alas, my poor friend Oswald, the prophecies say that I will die soon.

Oswald: Yes, my good sir. But how should this come about?

Janitor: Do you want the floor shined too?

(Suddenly, a huge tiger leaps at Lear)

Lear: Yah! What manor of devil spawn is this snarling foe that doth attack me?

Oswald: Shades of Scorpio! I think it doth try to kill you.

Lear: Get off me! Get off, I say!

Oswald: Janitor, help the good King.

(Janitor swings at tiger with his mop and mistakenly hits Lear in the face)

Lear: Fut! Knave fool! Where doth thou learn your aim - from a blind, degenerate, old man?

(King Lear is killed by the tiger) (The tiger dies of lung cancer)

Exit Oswald

(Janitor stays behind to clean up the mess)

Curtain Falls

Anthony looked towards the pompous critic. A stony silence separated them into East and West Germany. You could get shot trying to get over that silence.

"Anthony," the pompous critic inhaled deeply, his pipe working overtime. "What is it you expect from this manuscript?"

Anthony paused to think things over.

"What do you mean?" he asked, being careful.

70

"Do you want women, money, fame, prestige, a life in academia?" the pompous critic puffed.

"Well," Anthony wavered, "not all at once!"

"Ah," the pompous critic smiled. "You basically want to profit from a manuscript that may well throw Shakespeare's entire career into disrepute?"

"No," Anthony shook his head, "I don't want ..."

"Then what do you want?" the pompous critic interrupted him. "If this is an authentic manuscript – and that's a big if," he was careful to emphasize – "then you could very well destroy his reputation merely for your commercial gain."

"Well I ..."

"Haven't thought of that, have you?" the pompous critic raised his brows.

"No," Anthony tried to finish, "that's not ..."

"Then why continue with this charade?" the pompous critic cut him off. "Why are you doing this?"

"Well, I ..."

"Why?" the pompous critic jumped in.

"To have fun," Anthony blurted.

"Fun?" the pompous critic's voice went up an octave. "You want to have fun?"

"Yes," Anthony held up his manuscript. "I think these bits and bobs are fun."

"Fun are they?" the pompous critic countered. "So, you're displaying a complete lack of respect for not only Shakespeare but the opinions of the entire critical establishment of which I am a proud member?"

"I'm not too worried," Anthony began, "Shakespeare is already popular enough – I don't think my little manuscript will change that. Nor do I think it will stop you critics from meeting for coffee, attending fancy parties and lecturing about the minutia of life."

"You're not going to respect his legacy," the pompous critic sputtered –"or the critical establishment?"

"To be honest," Anthony replied, "Shakespeare is the Brussels sprouts of the literary world."

"What do you mean by that?" the pompous critic said, after a brief pause for reflection.

"I don't really like him," Anthony continued; "I'm just forced to have him because he's supposed to be good for me."

"You're hardly the ideal person to deliver this manuscript to the world," the pompous critic shook his pipe at Anthony. "Your quest for fun has blurred your judgment and may do more damage than good. Furthermore, owing to your complete disregard for convention, I think you may well have tinkered with these so-called unproduced plays just so your readers can enjoy a cheap laugh!"

"Your analysis is hasty, unfounded and poorly judged," Anthony stood tall.

"You're not wearing any trousers," the pompous critic replied.

Anthony sat back down.

"Well then," Anthony began, "let's hear some more of the manuscript, shall we?"

"If you insist," the pompous critic searched his cardigan for more tobacco. "Let's get this over with."

The following piece is a letter which Shakespeare had addressed to someone named Roderick, but apparently he never mailed it.

Seventh of September, 1601
Dear Beloved Roderick,

Yesterday I had the strangest experience, so strange that I feel I must relate it to you. As it were, I awoke from my afternoon nap and immediately realized that I was dreaming. Yes, I was completely conscious of the fact that I was dreaming. The colours within my room became unbearably bright, as I flung back the sheets. I went over to my window and opened it. The cool afternoon air cascaded over my naked body and filled me with a deep, profound longing.

While standing there, watching the snow fall, I realized that an elderly woman was looking up at me with the most curious expression on her face. Knowing that this was but a dream, I felt no embarrassment. In fact, I embraced the shear absurdity of the subconscious experience by flinging myself out the window. I landed on the cold hard ground, a few feet from the elderly woman. Of course, I was not injured, however, I was surprised at how realistic the impact seemed.

By this point, the elderly woman's screaming had reached an apex. I was suddenly overcome with naughtiness. I began to rub my naked body up against her. I screamed terrible insults into her ear, as she went into convulsions of screaming and crying. She fell to the ground and I dashed off towards the market. Shop keepers were speechless, and astonished faces appeared at every window, as I raced along the crowded streets. The snow, the wind, the bustling crowds of carollers and shoppers did not daunt me.

I have never felt so alive as I did in that dream, my good friend Roderick. I felt immortal - completely lawless. I had not a care in the world, unlike my waking state. So do not hold it against me, my good friend, when I tell you that I somehow ended up riding bareback on a tremendous pig! What playful nonsense! Could you imagine me - naked on the back of a pig?! I rode round and round the stable on the crazed beast, creating quite a stir with the stable hands, before I realized that I had interrupted an agricultural festival which was being attended by the Royal Family.

Regardless, I kept the palace guards and the stable hands at bay using a long leather bullwhip. Never had I possessed such energy! In between fighting off the enraged mob, which was rapidly gathering around me, I managed to run up into the audience and place a young newlywed in a compromising position. In a burst of playfulness, I raced into the horse stable and proceeded to tear the clothing off of a terrified young boy who was washing a horse.

The growing mob was close behind, but in my dream I moved, with speed and grace, across fields and through allies and gardens. Although aware of my nakedness, I did not feel weary, yet I was conscious of the fact that my dream may soon end. To make the most of my situation, I stepped out of character. I broke into a church and severely beat a priest. I ran like a wild man, up and down the pews, as the nuns hid their faces and cried out in fear. The mob burst into the church and captured me.

My dream then became more fragmented, as they carried me off. I only saw flashes of startled looks. Some of the people I may have recognized as actual associates of mine in the waking world. There was plenty of screaming and yelling. Public opinion did not seem to be in my favour. But I felt no guilt. It is lucky that a man cannot be found accountable for those sinister impulses he submits to in dreams.

Realizing that I was in a courtroom, I began to scream an endless stream of obscenities. To get a rise, I confessed to witchcraft and devil worship. I confessed to various carnal sins, too lewd too be mentioned in a waking state. I confessed to thievery and murder. I confessed that the dream state is a man's only true source of freedom where nothing is questioned and everything is permitted. At that point, a guard approached me and slapped me hard across the face. The judge informed me that I was very much awake.

My good, dear friend Roderick, I would greatly appreciate it if you could collect one thousand pounds and come forth in a carriage as soon as can be allowed. I will be waiting for you at the front gate. The officials are gracious enough to let me wait there for you. They now know me well. I am forever indebted to you.

Yours Without Question,
William Shakespeare

P.S. Please try to remember to bring me some clothing.

The pompous critic laughed out loud.

"You liked it?" Anthony smiled.

"Preposterous!" the pompous critic cried. "I think Shakespeare was a bit more subdued than that."

"It came with this photo," Anthony held up a photograph of Shakespeare, as evidence. "Surely a photograph of Shakespeare is as rare as hen's teeth."

"You'd be correct," the pompous critic leaned forward, "because cameras didn't exist in the seventeenth century – and that's a photo of Paul Giamatti!"

"Oh," Anthony looked at the photo carefully. "Right – he was really good in 'American Splendor'."

"Enough fun and games," the pompous critic puffed on his pipe. "Let's get on to those plays of yours."

"I shall oblige," Anthony turned to a long-lost text.

"I can hardly wait," the pompous critic half-whispered.

The following excerpt is a scene that was originally to be included in Shakespeare's 'Hamlet'.

SCENE III: Enter Hamlet, Servant and Big Black Dog
Hamlet: Hark! My stomach growls, for I am hungry.
Servant: Why don't you have a Danish?
Hamlet: I don't like Danishes. Anything that comes from Denmark will spoil easily and right now there is definitely something rotten in the state of Denmark!
Servant: Alas, there is nothing in our cupboard but a bone.
Big Black Dog: ARF!
Hamlet: Shall I eat the bone?
Big Black Dog: GROWL!
Servant: Maybe you should not.
Hamlet: Yes, that is best. Nick-knack, paddy-whack, give the dog a bone!
Exit Hamlet and Servant
(Dog turns to audience)
Big Black Dog: BARK! BARK! ARF!
Exit Big Black Dog

Anthony looked up from his manuscript. He was greeted with an uncomfortable silence, broken only by pipe smoke snaking its way upwards.

"Well?" Anthony ventured.

"Anthony," the critic sighed, "that was a piece of shit."

"Don't beat around the bush," Anthony demanded. "How do you really feel?"

"It doesn't inspire confidence in the rest of the manuscript," the pompous critic slowly shook his head.

"Well then," Anthony responded with confidence, "I guess you better listen to the rest of the manuscript before you pass judgment."

"If you insist," the pompous critic sighed. "Read on, young

man – read on."

This final excerpt was originally intended to be the climactic scene of Shakespeare's brilliant play 'Julius Caesar'.

(Caesar stands atop a gigantic tower on the embattlement. He revels in his victory over the barbarian hordes by enjoying a slice of chocolate cake. He sees Brutus walking along the base of the tower. Caesar calls down to him.)

Caesar: Brutus! Wait there, my friend, and I will bring you down a piece of this delicious chocolate cake.

Brutus: What?

Caesar: I said wait there and I will bring you a piece of cake!

(Brutus does not appear to hear Caesar. He walks away from the tower and heads home to relax after a hard day's fighting. Feeling as though Brutus has blatantly ignored him, Caesar becomes infuriated and races to his telephone. He dials Brutus's number and someone picks up the phone on the other end.)

Brutus: Hello.

Caesar: Brutus, is that you?

Brutus: Yes, it is. Who are you?

Caesar: I am Caesar - your emperor! Why did you not wait for me below the tower when I told you that I was bringing you down a piece of chocolate cake?

Brutus: I couldn't hear what you were saying. I thought you called me a "flake". I felt embarrassed, so I went home.

Caesar: You fool - I was yelling "cake"! I just wanted to give you a piece!

Brutus: Well, next time you should yell louder to avoid hurting your friend's feelings!

(Brutus hangs up)

Caesar: That little bastard!

(Caesar slams down the phone)

Caesar: Well, I guess I'll just eat all of this delicious chocolate cake myself!

(A wretched, old hag - who is clothed in rags and carries a walking stick - enters Caesar's chamber)

Wretched, old hag: Beware of the chocolate cake! For it is full of cholesterol and saturated fats!

Caesar: Who are you to tell me what to eat? You wretched, old hag - who is clothed in rags and carries a walking stick - I am the emperor! Therefore, I am obliged, by divine right, to eat whatever flavour of cake I choose!

(Caesar ignores the wretched, old hag - who is clothed in rags and carries a walking stick - and continues to devour the chocolate cake. As a result, his cholesterol level rockets upward. He dies of a massive heart attack.)

Curtain Falls

"How was that one?" Anthony looked up.

The pompous critic was just returning from the toilet.

"Sorry," he said - "weak bladder. What were you saying?"

"Want me to read it again?" Anthony ventured politely.

"No, no," the critic shook his head. "I've really had enough of all this," he stood tall and gestured wildly around the flat. "None of it makes sense. The round objects, that cat - I don't approve of this at all!"

"I don't care what you think of my Shakespeare manuscript," Anthony started; "I didn't write it. But you have no business criticizing my flat - or my hobbies!"

"I'm afraid I do!" the pompous critic spat. "It's all context – context I say! It's my right as a critic to criticize all of it. This is all wound up in one big ball of twisted absurdity," the pompous critic shook his pipe at Anthony. "But I see right through it. I'm going to unravel that ball and expose all the string – weak string at that! Everyone's going to know about your so-called Shakespeare manuscript. The world will know that it is excrement – pure excrement! You'll never recover from my scorching review – your so-called literary endeavours are finished, Anthony Zen! Finished!"

The pompous critic put his pipe in his mouth and dragged his chair towards the door. Anthony was devastated. The critic's harsh words were little vampires, draining away his excitement and enthusiasm. What started as an honest attempt to entertain a Shakespeare-mad public with a rare find had ended in pieces around his feet. The critic, almost at the door, was on route to deliver his verdict to the world outside. Anthony had no choice now but to await sentencing - but his cat was having none of it!

Monty had pulled one of the oldest tricks in the seemingly

infinite book of tricks for cats – he pretended to be asleep. All this time, he had one half-opened eye on the pompous critic; probably because there was a scent of tuna fish wafting from his cardigan, but maybe he didn't trust the critic and was watching out for Anthony. It was a difficult decision for a cat – maintain his watch for a sense of tuna or a sense of duty? Only nature could tell which track this train would depart on – and depart it did!

Like a bolt of lightning, Monty leaped into action. Of course, he wasn't as fast as a bolt of lightning – that would be too much. Let's just say his speed lay somewhere between an enraged cat, hyped up on the scent of tuna, and a bolt of lightning. That's the ticket; a ticket aboard a speeding train departing on track two – 'sense of duty'. The pompous critic cried out. Monty's claws sunk deep into his cardigan – of possible historical significance. The critic leaped up and tried to shake him, but Monty's claws clamped onto him like he was a piece of tuna. This was one train that wasn't returning to the station.

The pompous critic shrieked and ran around the room, his pipe flailing in the air. Jumping up and down, he tried to reach back and remove Monty. He knocked into furniture and stumbled into walls. Round objects rolled from the high shelves, hitting the pompous critic on the head, as if by grand design. The pompous critic, an old man with a weak heart, flailed madly, tears running down his cheeks. Crying out, he swung back and forth, but Monty was steadfast. Realizing what he had to do, Anthony jumped up. He couldn't let this continue without acting. He raced to the drawer, the cupboard and then the refrigerator. Rocketing back to his chair, he collapsed into it. Positioning the bottle opener just so, he popped the cap of his beer. He tore open a bag of crisps. Assuming a comfortable position, he watched the action unfold whilst munching crisps and guzzling beer.

It's hard to say how much longer it went on, this battle between cat and critic. Suffice to say, the pompous critic's cardigan was of even more historical significance and Anthony had just run out of crisps. Sensing that the pompous critic's visit was over, Anthony held the door open. Monty jumped off the pompous critic's back. The pompous critic, visibly shaken by the attack, dragged his chair out into the corridor as quickly as his old bones would allow. Anthony watched him drag the chair towards the elevator, its heavy wooden legs scraping across the floor. Just before the pompous critic disappeared into the elevator, Anthony issued a final parting shot.

"Put that in your pipe and smoke it!" he hollered, just as the elevator door closed.

Anthony returned to his chair and flipped through his prized 'Shakespeare Unplugged' manuscript. The pompous critic's smoke could trouble someone else now; it was no concern of Anthony's. Monty jumped up on his lap. The cat's gentle ticking was strangely soothing. Who knew what the future held now? Again, Anthony was not concerned. He was at peace. Reading through the plays, gently stroking his eccentric feline companion, he laughed out loud at the absurdity of it all. The plays were pretty funny too.

How Anthony's Parents Met

Howard Zen was a bus driver by profession. He found it a rather boring occupation. However, as a bus driver, he was able to enjoy several job-related perks that the rest of society surely envied. For example, once in a while he'd try to run over the odd cat - some of which he'd actually find trying to cross the road - or he'd race along the beach, run a few red lights and maybe even pick up a passenger or two. He tried to remain humble about his prestigious duties as a public servant, but his modest lifestyle was shattered when he first laid eyes on Miss Temple Shirley.

The moment Temple stepped onto Howard's empty bus, he knew right away she was the woman of his dreams - as a matter of fact, he was fast asleep at the time. Lucky thing too; being asleep, he left the door wide open. He usually kept it locked to avoid something unfortunate happening – like passengers getting on board. Fortunately, on this occasion, Howard's forgetfulness allowed Temple to enter into his humble life. He was immediately attracted to her strong fashion sense. She wore a green pig-skin Victorian dress, blue army boots and an immaculate sombrero. She carried a stylish purse that was moulded into an incredible likeness of Charles Bronson, in order to scare off envious sombrero lovers.

Howard Zen caught Temple's attention, due to the fact he was stark naked. Howard was, however, wearing his standard blue bus driver's hat and tie, which Temple considered a bold fashion statement. She smiled. Howard couldn't wait to validate her ticket. He wouldn't be giving her a transfer!

Temple got her ticket validated and started to light a cigarette. Howard kindly gestured to the 'No Smoking' sign. She'll have to give up on that habit, Howard thought.

Temple started searching for a seat. Howard slammed on the gas pedal and the bus tore away from the curb. Temple almost fell over.

"Sorry about that!" Howard hollered at Temple, who was steadying herself on a seat. "Had to act quickly before more passengers hopped on board."

Temple eventually sat down seven seats behind Howard.

The attractive young couple immediately dove into lengthy conversation, although they had to scream and yell in order to be heard over the bus engine. It is always best to get the screaming and yelling over with early on into a relationship. Continuing with their screaming and yelling, Temple munched on pineapples and avocados, which she had stored in her sombrero.

Howard and Temple discussed a wide variety of completely interesting topics, such as how to minimize the amount of crumbs on fresh toast and the effect of global warming on people with bad breath. The couple wished the day would never end, as Howard carefully guided the bus through the busy city streets and Temple skilfully removed pieces of avocado that became lodged between her teeth.

But then, without warning, a strange twist of fate occurred, sealing the future of this fun-loving couple. Due to an error in Howard's calculations, and partially due to over-inflated tires, the bus deviated from its regular route and accidentally rocketed into outer space, where it began to orbit the Earth.

Initially, this was a bit of a shock to Howard and Temple, considering that he was to return the bus after work and she had a hair appointment scheduled for sometime in the next five years. Surprisingly enough, the young couple gradually adapted to life in outer space; it took them about three weeks. After those first three weeks, Howard and Temple really got to know each other. They decided to get married. However, there didn't seem to be anyone on the bus who could marry them.

In an act of desperation, Howard tore through the lost and found box at the front of the bus. Luckily, he discovered a Catholic priest that someone must have left behind during rush hour.

"Will you marry us?" asked a hopeful Howard.

"Are you Roman Catholic?" replied the curious priest.

"No, I'm Howard Zen."

"Close enough," the priest pulled out his Bible. "Let's get this over with."

Thus, Howard and Temple Zen became husband and wife, respectively. The wedding aboard the orbiting bus was about as exciting as it could be, considering it was rather poorly attended. Apparently, no one on Howard's side of the family was keen on space travel and everyone on Temple's side of the family was in jail after an enormous riot at a local bowling tournament. It was just as well anyway; the wedding was cut short by a lengthy meteor shower and a visit from a large black monolith who wasn't on the guest list.

After the festivities wound down, Howard put the Catholic priest back into the lost and found box. However, the priest initially resisted; he disliked sitting beside a copy of 'The Catcher in the Rye', which someone had left behind on the bus. After a brief scuffle, Howard was able to convince the priest to return to his humble abode. With the priest finally back in the box, Howard and Temple could feel free to enjoy their marriage. Needless to say, there were lots of tickets to be validated.

In the years that followed, Howard and Temple were as happy as any young couple orbiting Earth in a bus. Howard, in an effort to make the bus more liveable, constructed a swimming pool out of some cement mix, steel girders and plastic raincoats which he found beneath the seats of the bus. He also set to work on a complete poolside patio arrangement constructed from large wooden planks that the priest, in an effort to get comfortable, kept tossing out of the lost and found box.

Temple was also quite busy removing large bags of topsoil from the luggage compartments, in order to create a sizeable vegetable garden. The garden was an instant success. With the addition of Howard's gazebo, crafted from several walking canes and a few dozen umbrellas, it became aesthetically pleasing as well.

Within the garden, Temple was able to grow turnips, broccoli, radishes, pickles, pumpkins, tomatoes, hash browns and kiwis. Howard greatly appreciated the addition of vegetables to his diet; for the last three years aboard the orbiting bus, he had been eating nothing but Nutella and tuna on crack wheat bread. Besides the vegetable garden, Temple was also preoccupied with her flock of sheep, which grazed freely about the bus. The sheep made excellent pets; however, neither Howard nor Temple could explain where they came from.

When Howard and Temple Zen finally completed all of their renovations, they were amazed at how much they had accomplished inside a bus that looked rather small from the outside. Yet, regardless of all the luxuries aboard their orbiting bus, they still craved excitement. It didn't seem as though the indoor pool and patio, vegetable garden, gazebo, flock of sheep and the priest in the box were enough to keep them occupied. To relieve mutual frustration and impending marital stress, Howard suggested they take a honeymoon vacation.

"Hey honey," he spoke up, with sudden enthusiasm. "We never really had a honeymoon, so let's go to Las Vegas and catch Wayne Newton's act."

"And just how are we supposed to do that?" Temple asked.

"Easy," Howard replied, "we'll use a really big net!"

So Howard directed the bus towards Las Vegas. Soon afterward, the fun-loving newlyweds had captured Wayne Newton and his band, as they departed from 'The Big Shiny Club' where they performed for a lethargic crowd of sun-burnt, over-weight tourists wearing zodiac chains and flowered shirts. The bus returned to its orbit around the Earth.

At first, Howard and Temple found it extremely exciting having a big Las Vegas entertainer in their very own bus. However, after just a few days aboard the orbiting bus, some of Wayne Newton's band members started to complain about allergic reactions to Temple's sheep. To make matters worse, Wayne himself was so terrified of Temple's Charles Bronson purse he constantly broke down and cried. Howard had no choice but to return the allergy-stricken, Charles Bronson-fearing entertainers back to Las Vegas. At this point, it became obvious to the young newlyweds that outer space just wasn't everyone's cup of tea.

After five years spent orbiting the Earth on a bus, both Howard and Temple grew rather restless. Life on the bus was becoming rather dreary - to say the least - and no one ever visited the relatively young couple. Even the large black monolith stopped visiting them, because the sheep kept peeing on it.

None of the modern contrivances Howard and Temple had aboard the bus could alleviate their growing feelings of anxiety. At first, they were excited by the discovery of the DVD player and the television, in the lost and found box which the Catholic priest called home. Initially, it was difficult to intercept any television stations. However, Howard was able to rig a functional satellite dish using Temple's sombrero. As a result, the young (but not as young as before) couple were able to enjoy a wide variety of fine television programs, such as 'Monday Night Deep Sea Diving' and re-runs of 'Diff'rent Strokes'.

Sometimes Howard and Temple would visit the priest in the lost and found box, which was still located at the front of the bus. The priest built himself a beautiful home out of lost lunch boxes. It took him quite a while to construct his dream home. He had to clear away all of the lost mittens, scarves, wool hats and purses with the aid of a large digger that some absent-minded construction worker left on the bus. Howard was amazed at how much stuff could fit into the lost and found box. He found it extremely interesting, searching through all the articles that people left behind.

Howard and Temple especially enjoyed the priest's company around Christmas, since they exchanged gifts. Over the years, the Zens had given the priest garden-fresh vegetables, tuna and Nutella Christmas cake and Temple's Charles Bronson purse, which the priest promptly returned - he was terrified of it. The priest gave the young (or so they were five years ago) couple a microwave oven, designer clothing, top secret CIA files and anything else that was cluttering up his box.

Aside from Christmas, life on the orbiting bus was becoming increasingly mundane. In an effort to alleviate his boredom, Howard decided to grow a beard. He kept the beard in a little pot, near the front window. He watered it every day, hoping it would grow long enough so he could actually try wearing it.

As usual, Temple tried to generate excitement through gardening and her new passion: sheep shearing. Before long, she was using the collected wool to knit several stylish items such as house coats, suspenders, bathing suits and an attractive 'welcome' mat - in case they ever got a visitor. As a matter of fact, she was busy knitting a pair of wool pyjamas - with the likeness of William Shatner on the front - when she suddenly became aware of a completely terrifying entity peering in at her with loathsome, hungry eyes.

Temple could hardly find strength to scream, as the ungodly abomination encircled the bus. It was so enormous, so hideous in design, that it defied all mortal forms of description and provided an excellent narrative hook for the next paragraph.

Temple was instantly seized by a paralyzing fear. She dropped the pyjamas; a spectacular crashing sound echoed throughout the bus, as they struck the floor and shattered into a million pieces. This was unusual, considering the pyjamas were made out of wool; but when you're orbiting the planet Earth in a bus, anything is possible. The sound of the breaking pyjamas brought Howard running to his wife's side.

"What's the matter, honey?" Howard cried, reaching out to her.

Temple could hardly answer him. In her state of awesome fear, she remained completely motionless - yet quivering - with the pieces of shattered wool pyjamas scattered around her feet. Somehow, Temple found the strength to raise her arm. She pointed out the nightmarish monstrosity which briefly claimed her sanity and was now preparing to attack the bus.

"There it is!" Temple screeched, motioning towards one of several windows on the bus. "A giant clam!!"

Howard dashed to the windows, half hoping his wife was mistaken, but also afraid to view what he thought might be converging on the bus. Howard's fears proved to be legitimate. The bus was being attacked by a dreaded interstellar mollusc!

"Fasten your seat belt," Howard cried. "I'm assuming evasive manoeuvres!"

"What seat belt?" Temple looked around the bus.

"Oh, right," Howard paused, fastening *his* seat belt. "Hold on to the sheep!"

He lunged to the controls of the bus and immediately steered away from the obviously famished mollusc. Using all the skill he could muster, he successfully dodged the endless streams of water which the mollusc spat at the retreating bus. Suddenly, he remembered the bus was equipped with photon torpedoes - for intergalactic emergencies such as this.

"Take cover, sweetheart," Howard shouted excitedly. "I'm putting windshield-wiper deflectors on maximum and I'm arming photon torpedoes! We're going to give that monstrous, water-spitting bivalve a taste of its own medicine!"

Howard fired the photon torpedoes at the immense mollusc which threatened his humble bus. The windshield-wiper deflectors seemed to be holding up against the abomination's continual spitting. In the heat of the fantastic battle, the Catholic priest leaped out of the lost and found box and began to panic.

"2001," he shrieked - "A Space Oyster!"

The crazed priest flung open the door of the bus and leaped

out into space. The cabin pressure immediately dropped. Several thousand pairs of lost mittens were sucked from the lost and found box and flew out the door, following the suicidal priest to his uncertain destination.

"That fool!" Howard cried, hoping to be heard over the sound of air being sucked into space. "Doesn't he realize that there's no oxygen out there? And not only that, it's really dark! He just went against one of the cardinal rules of bus transit," Howard paused, while waging war against the bivalve menace. Temple took shelter beneath the flock of sheep which joined together to form a giant pyramid for defensive purposes. "When you're riding on the bus," Howard continued, his hat and tie being pulled towards the door, "always stay in your seat and don't stick your arms out the windows, or stand near the door, when the bus is being attacked by an enraged extraterrestrial invertebrate!"

"The welcome mat!" Temple cried, as it got sucked out into space.

"Sorry, dear," Howard swerved the bus left and right. "These things happen."

"I'll start knitting a new one," she got out her knitting needles.

"OK".

With the reflexes of an enraged wombat, Howard unbuckled, leaped up and slammed the door shut - before all of the oxygen was drained from the bus. He secured the door and regained control of the bus. Temple, hidden within the sheep pyramid, was in a perfect position to knit. There was certainly no shortage of wool. She got to work immediately.

Continuing with his attempts to ward off the ensuing menace, Howard realized that the photon torpedoes didn't seem to be affecting the fiendish mountain of shellfish.

"Damn!" he screeched. "These photon torpedoes are bouncing off of that monster's calcareous shell like peanuts off of a Sumo wrestler!" He paused to consider the alternatives. "If only I could get a shot at its adductor muscle when it opens its mouth!"

"What colour would you like?" Temple cried out, hoping to be heard from within the sheep pyramid.

"What?" Howard hollered.

"What colour would you like the welcome mat?"

"What colours do you have?" Howard wiped his brow, firing a few more photon torpedoes.

"Only white," Temple nudged a sheep aside so she could hear.

"That will do!"

And then a brilliant plan entered Howard's head. He turned to his wife for assistance.

"Temple," he hollered, with desperation in his voice, "Check the bottom of all the seats and collect as much chewing gum as you can - and hurry!"

"I'll finish the welcome mat later," she crawled out from within the sheep pyramid.

"OK".

Setting the welcome mat aside, Temple faithfully collected as much gum as she could and brought it up to Howard.

"Here's the gum!" Temple shrieked enthusiastically, upon completion of her mission. "I also found this half-eaten Milky Way bar. Do you want it as well?"

"No thanks, dear," Howard replied. "Chocolate is only effective against gastropods, such as snails and slugs. We're dealing with a bivalve here, so we'll have to use wads of chewing gum."

"How do you know so much about molluscs and outer space?" Temple inquired.

"I'm a professional bus driver," Howard replied - "I have to know these things!"

Howard placed the large ball of accumulated chewing gum into the garbage ejector and took aim at the gaping mouth of the molluscan atrocity. When the time was right, he fired the gummy projectile. It landed just in-between the creature's indestructible shells.

The effect of the gum on the attacking shellfish was instantaneous. It began to quiver and then, suddenly, it exploded with a spectacular visual intensity that would have made George Lucas envious.

"I did it!" Howard collapsed from exhaustion. "I successfully used my bus driving expertise to defeat a supposedly undefeatable foe. Now that that's over with, what else can possibly go wrong?"

"Well," Temple shrugged her shoulders, "I'm pregnant."

It was a glorious day, indeed. Not only had Howard proven his manliness in battle against a gigantic bivalve, but he was also about to become a father. Knowing full well that a bus orbiting the planet Earth was no place to raise a child, Howard and Temple Zen mutually decided to move back to Earth. Only then could they raise young Anthony Zen in a normal environment - although, in the end, it really didn't make much difference.

And so the Zen family lived happily ever after in their little humble bus on planet Earth. Few people came to visit them; things were pretty quiet during Anthony's toddler days. The only notable exception was the day a Catholic priest came plummeting down from the sky - followed by a few thousand pairs of mittens - and crashed through the roof of the bus, landing in the lost and found box. Shortly thereafter, a welcome mat landed outside the door – an open invitation to share in a life full of adventure.

Another Day at Work

Anthony Zen walked along the city streets with increasing speed, with the hope of arriving at work by 9:00 a.m. Examining his wristwatch, he estimated that the time of day lay somewhere between 8:59 and 9:00 a.m. Of course, mere estimation would have to do. It was impossible for him to be exact regarding things of that nature. He could see nothing between the black dashes that marked each minute. Regardless, he figured that he still had plenty of time to get to work, providing that he didn't stop for something interesting along the way. Of course, as fate would have it, something of interest presented itself in short order.

While passing by a large city park, Anthony noticed several elderly men perched up on benches, feeding the birds, while several children, frightened looks on their chubby faces, ran from the playground, screaming and crying. He paused to see what was startling the children. He couldn't immediately determine the cause of all the commotion. The children raced past him with such speed that he couldn't question any of them. When the stampede finally died down - leaving behind it empty swings, abandoned toys and half-eaten snacks - he had his first chance to completely survey the area. Only then did he notice the man dressed in a space suit, complete with bulbous helmet, slowly making his way through the park playground. Even though he was a fair distance away, Anthony could hear his oxygen tank hiss with every breath he took.

"What are you doing over there?" Anthony called out to the spaceman.

The spaceman stopped and looked around the park, as if the question was directed at someone else. Seeing that there was no one else around him, the spaceman motioned with his thumb to make sure Anthony was referring to him.

"Yes, you!" Anthony hollered impatiently.

The spaceman, apparently startled at being discovered, suddenly twisted round and tried to run away. However, no sooner had he turned to run than he tripped over his own two feet and stumbled to the ground with a thud.

Anthony kept his eye on the spaceman, laying there in his

silver spacesuit, sprawled across the park grass. He expected him to get back up, but after a few minutes he made no such attempt. In fact, he did not move at all.

Thinking that the spaceman was dead, Anthony continued on his way to work. It would be a precious waste of time for him to stare at a dead spaceman for any longer, especially since it was rapidly approaching 9:00 a.m.

Without further distractions, Anthony arrived at work - promptly at 9:00 a.m. Walking into the office, he noticed that Miss Java, Meathead and Barney Blackfeet were all completely glued to their respective issues of the morning newspaper. Their expressions of shock and disbelief captured Anthony's curiosity. He purposely passed by them slowly, so he could catch the front page story. He thought he saw something about an astronaut, written in large bold type.

"Did you hear what happened?" Meathead suddenly lowered his paper, embarrassing Anthony for being so nosey.

"No," Anthony moved towards the coffee maker, "what happened?"

"The famous astronaut, Hugh Marshall," Miss Java lowered her paper, almost in tears - "they sent him up in a rocket to Mars last night and now he's been found dead!"

"Where did they find his body?" Anthony frowned suspiciously, a pot of coffee caught in suspended animation above his cup.

"It doesn't say," Barney broke in, scanning his newspaper. "And it doesn't mention how he died either!"

"Seems odd to me," Anthony thought aloud, pouring his coffee almost unconsciously, distracted by other thoughts.

"There's a rational explanation behind his death, I'm sure of it," Meathead began. "A million things can go wrong in outer space. Personally, I think he was probably enjoying a roast beef sandwich, while walking along the dunes on Mars, when a stray meteorite struck him on the head."

"I don't think it happened like that at all," Miss Java shook her head. "He was probably conducting scientific experiments on a large rock formation - while enjoying a cup of coffee, of course - when he accidentally inhaled a poisonous gas!"

"That's not it at all!" Barney laughed. All eyes were on

Barney now. What was his hypothesis? He had a real authoritative air about him that made people take notice and listen, or maybe it was just those dresses he always insisted on wearing backwards. "He was probably standing atop a speeding asteroid," he began, becoming quite dramatic, "when an evil alien entity seized hold of his life-force. I bet that beneath that spacesuit he was wearing a dress!"

"Maybe it was a combination of all three scenarios," Anthony concluded on a sarcastic note, finishing up his last drop of coffee. His three co-workers, missing his attempt at humour and being very wrapped up in the entire issue, looked at each other momentarily and nodded in agreement.

"Far be it from me to burst your bubbles," Anthony laughed out loud, shaking his head. He couldn't help himself.

"Who do you think you are?" Barney motioned towards Anthony. "Think you know better than us?"

"Yes," Miss Java became quite critical, "we've all shared our thoughts on Hugh Marshall, now how about you, Anthony? Please enlighten us with your brilliant hypothesis."

"Well I don't think you'd like to hear it, since you all think he's such a hero," Anthony seated himself at his desk, shuffling a few papers.

"That's a terrible excuse," Meathead snapped. "You'd better explain yourself."

"He's right," Barney nodded. "You're not getting off that easily."

"All right then," Anthony eased back in his chair, as they gathered at his desk "since you won't drop the subject, I think Hugh Marshall was a clumsy fool who died shortly after tripping and falling in the city park."

There was a moment of deafening silence which was comparatively pleasurable to the verbal onslaught that followed.

"Ridiculous!"

"The most absurd thing I've ever heard!"

"You're quite brave in your stupidity. I secretly admire you for it, although I can't believe I've just admitted to it in public. Damn!"

Arguments, innuendos, wild speculations - it took some time for things to subside. Relieved that everyone had returned to their desks, and hoping that the subject was dropped for good, Anthony concentrated on his paper shuffling. It was a difficult job, since so many sizes of paper presented themselves. Legal size, chart paper, graph paper, memos and photocopies - all requiring immediate shuffling. Would there be no end? As if he didn't have his hands full already, he couldn't get his mind off the fate of famed astronaut Hugh Marshall. He was angry, to say the least. He had been criticised unfairly by his fellow workers, who were completely ignorant regarding the truth behind it all. Feeling a need to vindicate himself, he considered phoning NASA and telling them that Hugh Marshall was not aboard last night's rocket launch to Mars. Instead, he apparently elected to stay on Earth and run around the city park in a successful attempt at scaring young children. However, the thought of reprisal prevented him from making the call. He feared that NASA would send people over to get him and give him a boring office job in Washington. He already had one of those, without even having to go near Washington!

Always ready to embrace change, Anthony stopped shuffling papers and began to sharpen a few pencils that happened to be lying around. He thought switching duties, even for a short time, would get the dead astronaut off his mind. But things of that nature are difficult for a young impressionable fellow to forget. To add to Anthony's distraction, his boss could be heard through the wall, snorting away within his office. He was probably watching a humorous cartoon. To add to the madness, Meathead refused to let the astronaut topic slip by.

"I wonder what types of meat astronauts eat," he purposely thought aloud, rubbing his chin.

"They can't eat meat!" Barney looked up from his desk. "They have to eat everything all mushed up - from a squeezable tube!"

"Well then," Meathead crossed his arms and leaned back in his chair, "they could eat pâté, couldn't they?"

Barney sat at his desk, leaning on his elbows, a thoughtful frown across his face. He suddenly sat up straight and nodded.

"I guess they could."

"Liver pâté would be a good choice," Meathead added. "It's good for you."

Barney turned back to his work, forcing Meathead to return

to whatever it is he does. Anthony was relieved. He'd had more than enough of astronauts. He had lots of paper shuffling to do before quitting time at 9:03 a.m. He could only finish if he had some peace and quiet.

"What type of coffee do you suppose astronauts drink?"

Anthony almost collapsed onto his desk. He shot an impatient glance at Miss Java.

"I bet they drink decaffeinated," she continued, "so they won't get jittery at the controls."

Anthony's stroke of bad luck had no end in sight. Barney leaped atop his desk, his backwards dress in full view, and began reminiscing about his old football days, his professional boxing stint and his childhood dream of becoming an astronaut.

Distracted and defeated, unable to accomplish the complex tasks laid out before him, Anthony stared blankly at his desk. He wished he'd never laid eyes on the astronaut who met his anticlimactic end in the city park, but would surely live on forever in posthumous fame. He checked his watch, out of shear optimism. It was 9:01 a.m. Obviously, it was going to be another long, gruelling day.

Anthony Goes to a Book
of the Month Club Meeting

It was a dreary Sunday afternoon and Anthony Zen was in Morrissey mode. Moping about, dragging his feet, unengaged with his surroundings, disappointed with boredom – his only friend. He searched for his Johnny Marr. There was nothing on the television; there was nothing beneath it either. In a fit of desperation, he called a few friends. He was unsuccessful. Regardless of how hard he yelled, they did not respond. His neighbour started banging on the wall. The neighbour below *him* banged on the ceiling. Then the neighbour below *him* banged ... and so on, and so on. Dogs barked in the distance. Birds flew. Anthony remained.

Silent and grey, the day wasn't going anywhere. It was like Uncle Mike after a wedding, lingering in the hall to search for lost change and half-finished drinks. Every family has an Uncle Mike. Anthony had to act. It was getting serious – Uncle Mike territory. Soon he'd be an overweight diabetic with no prospects. Heaven knew he was miserable now. His neighbour started banging on the wall. The neighbour below *him* banged on the ceiling. Then the neighbour below *him* banged ... and so on, and so on. Dogs barked in the distance. Birds flew. Suddenly, it struck him.

Anthony rubbed his head, checking for blood. He found a half-eaten banana. That shocked him; he didn't eat bananas. There was always something getting in his hair. He examined the banana. His head ached. It didn't add up. Bananas weren't known to cause head injuries. Coconuts, pineapples – maybe; but not bananas. Then it hit him. His neighbour started banging on the wall. The neighbour below *him* banged on the ceiling. Then the neighbour below *him* banged ... and so on, and so on. Dogs barked in the distance. Birds flew. Anthony noticed a trend: he was being hit on the head. He looked down and saw something lying at his feet. It was a book – *two of them*! He looked up and saw Monty perched atop a bookcase, looking mischievous - two books conspicuously missing from their spots. Monty had joined forces with gravity. Together, they propelled Anthony out of his doldrums. He bought his doldrums in Sweden. He wore them to bed every night.

Doldrums lay crumpled on the bedroom floor. His neighbour started banging on the wall. The neighbour below *him* banged on the ceiling. Then the neighbour below *him* banged ... and so on, and so on. Dogs barked in the distance. Birds flew. Uncle Mike ordered a cab. Anthony snatched his keys, a deckchair and a fluffy pillow - in case things got a bit dull. He raced out of the building, with purpose and intent – *and* a banana in his pocket.

Sprinting along the city streets, he realised he forgot to bring a book. No matter; he had a banana and a positive attitude (sometimes that's all you need). He tried to keep moving at all times; if he stopped, someone would plop down in his deckchair, demanding their shoes be shined. When he paused at an intersection, he avoided such a situation by sitting in the deckchair himself, waiting for the lights to change. With his pillow resting on his lap, he received generous donations from some of the passersby who assumed he was homeless; others thought he had a sleeping disorder. The fact that Anthony wasn't wearing any trousers only added to the effect. Everyone felt sorry for him, except for the police.

"I hope that deckchair is yours!" a policeman hollered, as Anthony raced past him.

"Where are you going with that banana?" someone else hollered.

Weaving in and out of the pedestrian traffic, Anthony came upon a common sight. All cities had them, whether they liked to admit it or not. Most people tried to avoid them. Bald heads, sandals, white robes, burning incense, chanting – you get the picture.

"Uh oh," Anthony muttered to himself – "toga salesmen!"

It was too late for poor Anthony. They pulled him aside. Four of them descended upon him.

"Do you want to buy an object?" one of them asked.

"What type of object?" Anthony asked, equally curious and relieved they weren't trying to sell him a toga; he wasn't a 'toga' person.

"This one I have in my hands," the man held it up to Anthony.

"What type of object is it?" Anthony looked it over.

"What do you mean?" the man replied. The other men gathered around to listen in. "It is an object - pure and simple."

Antony looked the object up and down.

"What's its name?" Anthony asked.

"It has no name," the man displayed it proudly. "It is just an object."

"Why does it need a name?" another man spoke up. Anthony realized that the four men all looked exactly the same. He honestly could not tell them apart.

"It is an object," another chimed in. "It is free."

"But don't *you* have a name?" Anthony asked the man holding the object.

"No, I don't" came the reply.

"Then how do you tell who's who?" Anthony looked the men over. "Some of you must have names."

"We don't," one said.

"We're free," noted another.

"We are objects," offered another.

"Who said that?" one asked.

"Said what?" another asked.

"He did,"

"Who did?"

"Him!" one gestured. "What's his face!"

Anthony, somewhat confused, set down his deckchair. He thought carefully about the situation. Pedestrians shuffled by; some paused to watch.

"I have a collection of round objects at home," Anthony announced.

"Do they have names?" one of the men asked. Anthony couldn't tell which one.

"No," Anthony shook his head.

"Why not?" another asked.

"They're just my round objects," Anthony offered; "they don't get names."

"But you called them 'round'", one man argued.

"That's just a description," Anthony countered.

"It's a label," another man said; "and therefore a name."

"But you need to describe things," Anthony pressed on with his point; "otherwise, how can you tell what's what?"

"I already know 'what's what'," the man holding the object smiled. "Do you want to buy an object?" he asked again.

"But how would you describe it," Anthony insisted.

"I wouldn't," the man shook his head; "it's just an object."

"Well guys," Anthony sighed, "I really need to get going."

"Where do you need to go?" one of them asked. The other three leaned in to hear.

"I'm going to a Book of the Month Club Meeting!" Anthony announced proudly, revealing his plan.

"Ah," the man with the object smiled, "you seek enlightenment."

"Yes," Anthony said, "my cat gave me the idea."

Anthony grabbed his deckchair and sped off, leaving confusion in his wake. He turned and waved goodbye to the four not-so-successful object salesmen.

"Anthony!" the man with the object hollered at him. "Set your objects free!"

"You just used a name!" the other three screeched.

"But he's not free yet!" came the response.

"Oh," the others mumbled.

Racing through the crowds, something struck Anthony as strange. It was the man with the object; it was something he said.

"Wait a minute," Anthony said aloud, embarrassed that it took him so long to realize it - "how much were they asking for that object?" It was now all too clear why the four men were such poor object salesmen. Anthony chose to forget about them and focus on his journey.

It didn't take long for Anthony to find where the Book of the Month Club met. All he had to do was follow the queue of balding men wearing wash-and-wear suits, clutching musty books and smoking pipes. Anthony didn't understand wash-and-wear. Did it make you look like last week's New York Times chasing after a street cleaner? He hadn't a clue, but his sense of smell never failed him. Mixed with tobacco smoke were distinctive notes of Old Spice and a slight musk finish that suggested an underground society where soap-on-a-rope was still in use. Clearly, these were men of a certain vintage.

Utilizing his youthful sprightliness to his advantage, Anthony snatched up his pillow and deckchair and jumped into the front of the queue. He was just too anxious to attend his first club meeting. Before long, he was actually inside the meeting place. However, his feelings of excitement were quickly doused; a sinister looking librarian was checking everyone for overdue books, at the front entrance.

The librarian's evil demeanour was substantially enhanced by the ominous security gate she operated. Whenever a person passed through the gate, with an overdue book in their possession, an alarm sounded and guards swarmed the perpetrator.

Anthony was unfortunate enough to witness the desperation first hand. There's always a bad apple who thinks he can circumvent justice, ruining the pie for everyone else. This particular bad apple tried sneaking through with an overdue book. The alarm sounded. Gasps flew. Heads turned. Knees knocked. The bad apple broke for cover. But they never fall far from the tree. The guards acted quickly on the librarian's orders. Drawing their weapons, they sprayed hot lead. Cries rang out. Several chairs were damaged. Posters advertising yoga lessons and free kittens – shredded! The bad apple was applesauce.

Watching applesauce seep out from a wash-and-wear suit, Anthony felt a pain, deep down in his heart. He took two antacid tablets. The pain went away. The guards, guns still smoking, gathered around the applesauce. Applesauce spat out his pipe and uttered his final words.

"It's not fair," he gasped, while the librarian confiscated his overdue copy of John Irving's 'The World According to Garp'. "I didn't get to finish it - it was *too damn long*!"

"Well, you should have just seen the movie!" the librarian sneered, with a wicked laugh. The guards swept applesauce away. Janitors came in to mop up the rest.

Anthony's feelings of remorse, for this unfortunate victim of the library system, soon vanished. He realized he was next in queue to step through the security gate. The librarian was returning to her post. He panicked, fearing the librarian would find out, through some sort of polygraph test, that he *did not have a book*.

Thinking quickly in his moment of absolute terror, Anthony looked down at his banana. Most men do, in moments of need. He noticed a colourful sticker adhering to its firm, yellow flesh. It read: Top Banana Farm 100 Ecuador Organic. Fondling his banana, before the librarian noticed, he carefully peeled the sticker free and pressed it onto the front left corner of his 'People are

Weird and Life is Stupid' t-shirt. There it remained – top banana indeed! Feeling confident, his pillow and deckchair at his side, he advanced towards the security gate.

"Who are *you*?" the librarian crossed her arms, looking Anthony up and down.

A guard squinted at the sticker.

"Top Banana?" he read aloud, looking towards the librarian for confirmation.

"A top-ranking *book official*," Anthony corrected him, proudly displaying the sticker, as if it was an I.D. badge.

The librarian glanced at the prestigious sticker adorning Anthony's t-shirt.

"Farm100?" she ventured with a dash of suspicion.

"Ah, yes ... where knowledge grows, between the books, row by row," Anthony stumbled.

"*Equador*?" shrugged a guard.

"Cheap labour," Anthony countered.

"Organic?" asked a guard, visibly confused.

"Yes, well ... in the scheme of things ...," Anthony choked, not knowing what to say.

"Is that a banana in your pocket?" the guard's question saved him.

"That's a personal question!" Anthony snapped.

"Pockets - *in your boxer shorts*?" a guard wondered aloud.

"What's with all the questions?" Anthony replied.

"He's right", the librarian suddenly chimed in, "Sorry, sir. Umm ... give us a moment, please."

"I suppose I could," Anthony collected himself, awkwardly adjusting his boxer shorts.

When they were out of range, the librarian and her guards huddled together, shooting nervous glances, making sure Anthony could not hear.

"Do you know who that is?" the librarian whispered.

"No, should I?" the turgid romance guard asked.

"Remember the rumour?" the librarian pressed.

"What - the library inspector?" the B-list celebrity memoir guard gasped.

"Yes!" she responded.

"The one who closed the central library?" the C-list celebrity cookbook guard ventured.

"Yes!"

"Who fires everyone?" asked the newspapers, education and politics guard. He had precious little to guard. Last in the library guard hierarchy, he was always last to contribute.

"Right!"

"That guy?" the turgid romance guard asked. He glanced at Anthony - boxer shorts, banana sticker, deck chair, pillow and something bulging out of his briefs. "He's an idiot!"

"That's just it," the librarian insisted.

"You mean he's *in disguise?*" the B-list celebrity memoir guard gasped. An overly dramatic type, he liked to gasp.

"Yes, he *wants* us to think he's an idiot – underestimate him," she whispered. "This is a *test!*"

"Ah, I see," the C-list celebrity cookbook guard ventured, as if by rote. He really had no idea what was up. As long as it was gluten free, he was all for it.

"So we have to play along," she continued.

"How so?" asked the newspapers, education and politics guard. The other guards rolled their eyes.

"Humour him," she said, with no respect for his logic. "Let's *pretend* to believe him. See what he does."

"OK," the newspapers, education and politics guard said cautiously, preferring to keep his response short, to avoid attracting undue attention.

"Our *careers* are on the line," she continued, eyeing the guards. "We have to play along!"

"How bad could it be?" asked the turgid romance guard.

"Exactly!" she nodded.

"It's just a few hours," the B-list celebrity memoir guard gasped.

"Right," the C-list celebrity cookbook guard agreed.

"What can possibly go wrong?" the newspapers, education and politics guard asked rhetorically, immediately regretting it.

"Agreed," she said. They all nodded and broke formation, returning to the gate.

"I'm so *very sorry*, Sir," she smiled nervously. "We had *no idea* you were coming."

She fell hook, line and little heavy lead thing for his imaginative trick – or so Anthony thought! She had completely ignored the fact that he was little more than a trouserless scallywag, lugging around a pillow and deckchair.

"Never have I experienced such an outrage!" Anthony interrupted her.

"Please accept our humble apologies!" she begged.

"We'll do everything we can to accommodate you," gasped the B-list celebrity memoir guard, diving into his role with gusto.

Playing the part for all it was worth, Anthony prepared his deckchair, fluffed his pillow and seated himself in the middle of the security gate. All eyes were on him. The librarian looked down in shame; but closer observation would have revealed fiendish eyes signalling to the security guards. Like a bad high school drama rehearsal, they burst into their roles, acting like they were lost for thought (easier for some than others), over-egging every gesture, fearing for their lives, insisting they'd never seen a top ranking book official before – the full Pacino. The club members, still waiting outside, were queued-up but not clued-in. Peeking through the front doors, they wondered what all the fuss was about.

"I came here to relax and enjoy a good book," Anthony bellowed, finding a comfortable position in his deckchair, "but what do I get instead - bullets flying everywhere! Chairs damaged! Free kitten posters – shredded! Kittens need homes!"

The security guards all looked down at their shiny black shoes. Seeing their reflections, some of them realized they forgot to shave.

"You should be ashamed of yourselves," Anthony shook a finger at the guards. "A Book of the Month Club Meeting is no place for gun play. And to think that some of you aren't even clean shaven!"

"We're all so sorry, sir," the librarian sniffled – the full Meryl Streep. "Just tell us what we can do to improve our service. We're open to suggestions. Unlike *lesser* libraries in the area, there's a suggestion box located near the elevators, if you would like to write down a few comments. We go through the suggestion box at the end of *each week*. Some of the better suggestions get posted on the notice board for everyone to see."

"There's lots of room for them," the newspapers, education and politics guard spoke out of turn, "now that the yoga and free kittens notices are gone." The other guards flashed him dirty looks.

"Don't make me get up out of my deckchair!" Anthony threatened the librarian, shaking his head. He was enjoying the authority he had gained; if only he knew it was all an illusion. He was ready to lay it on the line. "This is how it's going to work," he sat up, speaking so that everyone could hear.

"Now then," Anthony looked the guards up and down, "Thank you for your support to date." He turned his stony gaze to the librarian. "In light of recent developments, and in the interest of fairness, you must locate *at least three books* about nosey neighbours. Then ..."

"There's more!" the B-list celebrity memoir guard gasped, by force of habit.

"Yes!" Anthony straightened up, rubbing his chin. "Yes, there is! I want your best books about ... *barking dogs*. And another thing ..."

"More books?" the C-list celebrity cookbook guard asked.

"Yes, yes," Anthony snapped, "I want some books on bird flight and the secret of happiness."

"Would that be *two* books or *one*?" asked the newspapers, education and politics guard, feeling confident.

"I think ... that's .. *two*," Anthony thought aloud, slowly nodding. "Yes, two. Sounds like two to me."

The security guards suddenly broke into intensive conversation. Some of them, seizing the moment, pulled out electric razors and started shaving. Anthony, sensing he was losing control of the situation, fluffed his pillow, stood up and adjusted his boxer shorts. He stopped his banana from falling out.

"Silence!" he snapped. The security guards capitulated, returning their gaze to their shoes. "You mustn't dither. Books await. And when you're finished," he returned his attention to the librarian, "they will be helping *you*."

"Me?" she choked. "Do what?"

"You honestly have *no* idea what you *have* to do?"

"Yes sir," the librarian burst, "I think I do." She raced off to fetch a toolbox.

For his final request, Anthony demanded that the entire security gate be dismantled and removed. The security guards carried out the order. When Anthony's back was turned, the librarian silently motioned to the guards, begging them to take it up a notch – the full Nicholas Cage.

"WATCH as I unscrew these bolts!" cried the turgid romance guard.

"LISTEN as I saw this support beam!" gasped the B-list celebrity memoir guard.

"THRILL as the arch tumbles to the ground!" cried the C-list celebrity cookbook guard.

"CHEER as citizens flood into a well-managed public space!" announced the newspapers, education and politics guard.

Anthony felt they were acting strangely. Something was up. Before he could investigate, the doors swung open and everyone shuffled into the meeting, regardless of whether or not they had an overdue book. The balding men in wash-and-wear suits removed pipes from mouths. Some of them removed pipes from *other people's* mouths; they were a close-knit bunch. They cheered for Anthony and the justice he had performed. A neighbour started banging on the wall. The neighbour below *him* banged on the ceiling. Then the neighbour below *him* banged ... and so on, and so on. Dogs barked in the distance. Birds flew. Anthony beamed.

Anthony Goes to the Movies

Anthony Zen had no trouble locating the local cinema; the neon sign was glowing brighter than a swarm of fireflies chasing a flock of fluorescent turtles from their turf. However, once he reached the front of the cinema, he was faced with a difficult, challenging, perplexing, mind-numbing decision. Which movie should he see? The local cinema had several screens, so to choose amongst the cornucopia of celluloid experiences, the plethora of visual extravaganzas, the wasteland of big budget productions, would not be easy.

Gazing at the display of films before him, Anthony saw evidence of what he could expect during future trips to the cinema. For example, in cinema one, you could see Keanu Reeves playing Keanu Reeves in the movie version of Darwin's 'The Origin of Species'. In cinema two, one could pretend to enjoy Tom Cruise's new autobiographical film, 'Why I Think I'm so Damn Good'. Cinema three was featuring, for the third week in a row, Keanu Reeves playing Keanu Reeves in the movie version of Plato's 'The Republic'. Having no interest in any of these films, Anthony considered going into cinema four to see the 3-D documentary 'Things that Itch'. However, he was not really in the mood for anything intellectual either. The IMAX screen featured 'Terminator vs Alien vs Predator'. Intergalactic high jinks ensue when three rabble-rousers zip back and forth in time causing mischief and stretching logic and credibility to their limits. Not Anthony's cup of tea!

The only other choices facing Anthony included the animated feature 'Randolph Camel's Pancreas', based on the wildly popular Saturday morning cartoon about a wealthy camel's innards. Other screens featured Walt Disney's simultaneous releases of 'Bobbie and the Hob Nobs', 'Nobby the Bobbie' and 'Bobbie's Hobbies'; films which, depending on your persuasion, existed solely to flog hob nobs, support a police state or discourage masturbation – sometimes all three. Of course, in cinema ten, one could always see Keanu Reeves playing Keanu Reeves in the movie 'Keanu Reeves'. Suddenly, Anthony was surrounded! What was happening? His eyes shot back and forth. Nowhere to run to. Nowhere to hide. They were all around him – staring down with vacant eyes. Were they clones? Mutants? Genetically engineered beings from planet IKEA? Alas, it was far worse.

It was the *New Hollywood*, staring down from glossy posters. Perfectly pressed GAP clothing. Shirts pulled up to expose firm bellies. Perfectly coifed hair. Edgy tattoos. Air brushed faces. Own line of perfumes. What was this strange land? It was merely a celebration of the latest exploits of Bobbie Dana Taylor, Dana Bobbie Taylor and Taylor Dana Bobbie. Unless you saw them together in the same movie, you had to assume they were the same person. How Anthony missed the good old days of Bronson, Eastwood, Connery and Marvin - actors with faces that told a story. Actors with strong personalities. Actors people made a career out of impersonating. How could someone impersonate Bobbie Dana Taylor, Dana Bobbie Taylor or Taylor Dana Bobbie? The audience would probably think you were Dana Taylor Bobbie! Alas, the art of impersonation was dead, because real personalities were dead.

After quite some thought, Anthony decided to educate himself and see the 3-D documentary 'Things that Itch'. Feeling confident with his decision, he approached the ticket window and handed the cashier his hard-earned fistful of wrinkled, lumpy, dog-eared pound notes. Ticket in hand, he strolled over to the snack counter, intending to purchase some delightful, tasty, delicious, mouth-watering confections. He was met with cold indifference.

The young woman behind the counter stared into her smartphone. Unless she was searching for videos on how to use a cash register, she wasn't much use to Anthony. Anthony looked for other staff, to no avail. Catching a whiff of death, he peered over the counter and saw the naked body of a former employee. Dead for weeks, smartphone still in hand, his battery must have run out. Not knowing how to cope, let alone dress himself, he collapsed and died.

"Can I help you?" the manager asked, stepping over his dead employee.

"Yes, it's about time," Anthony replied. "She doesn't seem too keen to serve customers."

"Oh, her?" the manager began. "She doesn't work here. She got trapped behind the counter when her Google maps crashed. Anyway, what would you like?"

"I would like a large bag of popcorn," Anthony began, his hungry eyes searching through the edible items before him, "and a pure milk chocolate bar made from the finest, farm-fresh ingredients carefully blended in some village in Switzerland. And I'd also like a large cup of a refreshing, effervescing, glucose-saturated soft drink to go along with that."

"I see you're really taking advantage of National Descriptiveness Week!" replied the manger, suddenly animated.

Anthony forgot it was National Descriptiveness Week, but he played along anyway.

"The sky is really blue in a big sort of way," he threw his arms up, assuming a dignified tone. "The sun is round and it glows like a tremendous ball of ignited gases."

"Pretty wild stuff!" the manager beamed. "Now," he began in a more serious tone, "would you like some repulsive, oily, smelly, chemical-ridden, artificial butter substitute on your stale, dry, one-week old popcorn?"

"Yes, that would be completely fantastic in epic proportions!"

Just then, the owner of the cinema called out to Anthony.

"Hey kid!" he raced over. "Is there a tag on the back of your underwear?"

The embarrassment struck Anthony like a ton of bricks tied to a speeding train fired from the barrel of a gun. He forgot, once again, to wear his trousers. Regardless of this minor detail, he answered in a calm, collected manner.

"Well," he shrugged, looking away from him, "I never keep the tags. I always remove them, because they make my back itch."

"Congratulations!" the owner shook his hand. "You've just won a free package of Liquorice Nibs!"

"Yes, that's right," the manager interjected. "Anyone who doesn't have a tag on their underwear this week wins a free bag of Liquorice Nibs!"

For the first time in his life, Anthony did not feel embarrassed about forgetting to wear his trousers. He accepted the package of Liquorice Nibs and put them in his pocket.

"Wow!" the manager cried. "He's even got pockets sewn into his underwear!"

"I had my mom sew them in," Anthony modelled his look,

"because I'm always forgetting to wear my trousers and I need somewhere to put my wallet."

Before donning his 3-D glasses, and heading towards cinema four to see 'Things that Itch', Anthony thanked the owner for the prize. But his politeness was just a front for deep rooted discontent. He had to face the hard facts. The free confection was a meagre gesture, considering the outlandish cost of the popcorn he had just purchased. Yes, oil and gold are fine, but discover a popcorn field in your backyard and you have it made! Or do you? Sure, no other substance on the planet is so simple yet so expensive, but only a select few can reap the benefits of this precious treasure. Alas, harvesting, production, importing and exporting are all controlled with an iron fist by OPEC (The Organization of Popcorn Exporting Countries) - not to be confused with that other OPEC (Otters Prefer Electric Cuttlefish), a bizarre splinter group originating in a cave somewhere in Norway.

Anthony shook himself. What was he thinking? True, he had once again fallen victim to the tyrannical popcorn empire, but he forgot the cardinal rule of cinemas: EAT, DON'T THINK - the very foundation of any good capitalist society.

Dashing off, Anthony hoped he didn't miss the opening credits. Jogging through the lobby, not paying much attention, he unwrapped his chocolate bar and nibbled on his popcorn. It was inevitable. Other patrons saw it coming, but didn't cry out in time. They watched in horror. Popcorn flew everywhere. Anthony staggered back, shaking his head. He quickly appraised the situation. He had collided with an extremely, intolerably, exceedingly beautiful young lady who was exiting cinema two with an opened jar of peanut butter in hand.

"Your chocolate is in my peanut butter!" the young lady cried.

"Well," Anthony retorted, "your peanut butter is on my chocolate."

Anthony decided to take a chance and try some of his peanut butter covered chocolate.

"Mmm ... tastes great!" he shouted excitedly.

The attractive, peanut-butter-toting young lady tried some as well.

"Mmm ... you're right!" she nodded.

Anthony was about to ask the attractive young lady to marry him, when she seized his chocolate bar and raced out of the cinema, jar of peanut butter at her side. He was left feeling rejected and alone - now he was really in the mood for a 3-D documentary about things that itch. Captured in a moment of gloom and introspection, he chose not to pursue her. If only he had known that the attractive young lady happened to be Mary Reeses. She was going to take the peanut butter and chocolate - which Anthony helped to combine - and make millions selling it off as 'Reeses Peanut Butter Cups', while Anthony was to remain impoverished and alone.

Anthony quickly discovered that a big mouthful of environmentally unsafe popcorn and a handful of half-melted Liquorice Nibs, with a gulp of carbonated glucose to wash it down, was all he needed to forget about the attractive young lady. In fact, by the time he found a place to sit, and 'Things that Itch' began to play, he completely forgot about the girl, where he lived and who he was (he always got that way when he began to focus on the intricacies of a motion picture).

Anthony always sat on the left side of the cinema and in an aisle seat, due to his political inclinations – and if a fire broke out he'd be able to make a clean break for the door. No sooner had he sat down than a can of beer rolled past his feet, on its way downwards towards the screen. He heard a teenage couple giggling behind him. How fiendishly clever and original, Anthony thought to himself, his sarcasm meter pushing into the red; they've smuggled alcohol into the cinema.

Although they helped customers see the screen, Anthony always disliked the sloping floors in cinemas. Invariably, a variety of round confections and beverages came rolling or trickling down – troubling your shoes. Just then, another can of beer rolled by. The couple giggled uncontrollably. Anthony figured their fingers must be covered with butter – albeit the artificial kind. He was about to turn around and confront them when a baby rolled down the aisle in a pram. He watched it roll all the way down to the screen. The teenage couple took no notice of their lost baby. Judging by the noises they were making, and after a few drinks, they were already working on a new one.

Anthony tried to focus. However, he really disliked the first half of 'Things that Itch'; the film lingered on poison ivy and bug bites for far too long. He was also disappointed with the apparent complete lack of 3-D effects in the movie. However, when he had his 3-D glasses on, everyone around him appeared to be three-dimensional, so he figured he was getting his money's worth after all.

Of course, poor visual effects were only half the problem. Anthony also found it hard to hear, with all the noise at the back of the cinema. He did not bother to turn around and see what all the racket was about. If he did, he'd notice that the commotion centred on the activities of a colossal, blasphemous blob of seething, putrid sludge. The abomination had putrid gases escaping from its porous, haggish limbs. It was evidently created from a combination of fizzy drink residue, bubble gum, century old popcorn - of possible historical significance - and candy bar wrappers which had not been swept up off the cinema floor.

Now the hideous blob of cinema refuse was devouring patrons in the back row and belching loudly. No diplomat could reason with it. No weapon could faze it. No usher could get it to be quiet. Despite the racket, Anthony adjusted his 3-D glasses and tried to pay attention to 'Things that Itch'. However, his interest swayed once again; the movie began to linger on psoriasis and wool underwear.

It finally struck Anthony that he should *just leave*. He headed towards the glowing 'EXIT' sign to the left of the movie screen, without having to view the havoc at the back of the cinema. At the front of the cinema, he was surprised to see three vagabonds seated together, enjoying all the beer that had rolled down to them. At least it didn't go to waste, Anthony thought to himself.

"Is that your kid?" one of them motioned his can of beer at the pram.

"No," Anthony replied, halfway out the door. "Just follow the trail of beer up into the darkness and you'll find the proud parents."

Anthony's response caused quite a debate amongst the vagabonds. They thought he was speaking euphemistically.

Standing outside, Anthony felt relieved; he just could not stand the constant disruption. More importantly, he simply had to get out because the documentary 'Things that Itch' was about to discuss tags on the back of underwear. He would not be able to withstand the excruciating horror of having to watch that!

The Dirty Half-dozen

It was a hot, humid night. Smog fell over the city like a heavy wool blanket sprawled across one of those fancy silver dinner trays full of finger sandwiches, foreign cheeses and dessert squares - the likes of which you see at stuffy parties. It was so dark you couldn't see your own hand in front of you, but you could see someone else's – and it had your wallet. The acid rain didn't wash the garbage and trash off the sidewalks; it dissolved the sidewalks and left the garbage and trash behind.

He was single and working, which meant eight hour shifts, nine to five (what a way to make a living), sometimes nine to six in the p.m., five days a week. He could eat three to three-fifty a week, more with skim milk – in case you were wondering. He walked the whole city, up, down, don't make no difference to him – does to some. Some won't take croissants – hell, don't make no difference to him. We're all animals anyway – eat what you can get. All the animals came out at night: wombats, fireflies, tree tigers, giraffes, hippos, squirrels, turtles, dogs, cats. Someday a *real* rain will come and wash all the scum off the streets.

It was a hustle, but it kept him busy. Every day - do the hustle, do the hustle. Do the hustle. Oh, do it. Oh, do it. He *did* the hustle alright - day after day - and it got him jack squat. jack lived alone in a cardboard box down by the big rusty pipe – that's Mr. squat to you, punk! Yeah, it was one of *those nights*. Hello darkness, your old friend. That feeling in the pit of the stomach. The craving. Strong. Hard. Carbs and glucose. Forget the gluten, man! It was one of those nights when a trouserless young man with unusual hair gets an intense desire to ingest a freshly baked piece of dough that's carefully wrapped around a small column of air and covered in chocolate to make it complete. In other words, Anthony Zen craved donuts. Donuts!

Weaving through the congested, aching, feverish late night pedestrian traffic, 'Harry's Donut Store' was the franchise Anthony had in mind. 'Harry's Donut Store' was a popular meeting place. Harry often entertained his patrons by tossing wads of freshly baked dough up into the air. In a desperate attempt at creating proper donuts, the policemen frequenting the establishment quickly drew their revolvers and shot holes through the airborne dough. Of course, every once in a while, a customer or two were accidentally shot to death; but they had sat down for a coffee and a donut, so they should have known what they were getting into.

It didn't take long for Anthony to locate 'Harry's Donut Store'. The large neon sign was glowing brighter than a flock of fluorescent turtles chasing a swarm of fireflies from their turf. Anthony proceeded to the front door of the establishment and entered. He immediately realized why 'Harry's Donut Store' was also referred to as 'Dirty Harry's'. However, he wouldn't let this deter him; the dark, dingy, grimy atmosphere only added character to such an old local landmark - and it reminded him of his flat.

Anthony noticed - surprisingly - that there were no policemen present. There was, however, about a half-dozen members of a rough-looking motorcycle gang. Seated in the far corner, they watched Anthony closely - *too closely*. He quickly began to feel uncomfortable.

Anthony was certain that the motorcycle gang would harass him about his spiked hair, or the fact that he had forgotten - once again - to wear trousers. He could never understand why people where so fussy about little things like that. Ignoring the motorcycle gang's suspicious stares, he approached the counter to order some donuts.

"I'd like a half-dozen donuts, please," he began. "Two custard cream, one blueberry, two chocolate and a chocolate filled croissant."

"How incredibly filthy would you like those donuts?" the person behind the counter inquired.

Grime was so in. Tattoos, watch chains, skinny jeans and beards were *so last week*. To really fit in, you needed dirt – *real dirt*. You had to be living in it. Rolling in it. Breathing it. *Eating it.*

"Well," Anthony paused, "not very filthy. How filthy are they?"

"This one has mould all over it," the counter person proudly displayed the donut. "Hipsters can't get enough of these. They're flooding in from the suburbs – having given up on gluten free cupcakes long ago."

"No, I don't think I want that one," Anthony rubbed his chin, "but can you scrape the mould off it?"

"Of course not!" the counter person started, in a defensive tone. "That would ruin the carefully sculpted aesthetic value of the donut!"

"What's wrong with those donuts over there?" Anthony asked, while pointing. "Are they clean?"

"Not really; there's a bug on top of them."

"Can you remove the bug?" Anthony ventured.

"I suppose so," the counter person sighed. "But he's pretty colourful. Do you want to keep him as a pet?"

"No thank you," Anthony replied, fumbling for his money. "I keep a cat as a pet. Just give me a half-dozen donuts - without a bug."

Anthony handed the counter person a fistful of dollars and purchased a half-dozen of the cleanest looking donuts he could find. Turning to leave, one of the motorcycle gang members hollered an insult at him.

"You look like a stupid little goofy guy!" he barked. "I bet your dad wears army boots!"

The other members of the gang laughed callously.

"You're wrong!" Anthony retorted. "My mother's the one who wears army boots!"

"Oh, yeah?" started another gang member. "Well, you look like a stupid little goofy guy!"

"Didn't we already say that?" inquired another.

Anthony felt incredibly upset. He decided to give the gang of rowdies a piece of his mind.

"Look," he paused nervously, clutching his box of donuts, "I don't want any trouble, so why don't you guys leave me alone?"

"Why don't we leave you alone?" the leader of the gang mocked Anthony, approaching him with a switchblade in hand. "How about because we're uneducated, unemployed and unfashionable; and we haven't had a haircut, or a shower, in over a year!" The leader of the gang laughed sadistically, waving the knife in front of Anthony. "We're the good, the bad and the ugly - except without the good - and now we're going to beat you up so bad that ... you're gonna think ... that you got beat up - or somethin'."

As the knife-wielding gang member continued with his taunts and threats, Anthony became energized with an intense will to defend himself, in the tradition of the tremendous tree tigers which valiantly protect their bowls of porridge from curious turtles. Before the knife-wielding ruffian could recite the first scene from Shakespeare's 'Macbeth' - let alone blink - Anthony's reflexes kicked in. He quickly snatched a blueberry donut from his box and attacked the foul hooligan with it.

The leader of the bike gang screamed in agony and dropped his knife. Falling to his knees, he desperately tried to remove the sticky blueberry filling from the front of his 'I Killed Your Mum' t-shirt. The other gang members leaped up in a mixed state of fear, amazement and sobriety, because they suddenly realized that marijuana had yet to be legalized; however, they were also rather shaken by Anthony's sudden show of force.

Some of the gang members scurried towards the door, in order to avoid sharing their leader's hideous fate. Others wondered what on Earth a tree tiger was and if turtles really do eat porridge and, if so, who's making the porridge – the tree tigers? Whose bowls are they using? It didn't make sense. Anthony, on the other hand, would take no chances with these pathetic low-lives whom he would not trust with his grandmother's teeth, for fear they would get germs.

Anthony whipped out a custard cream donut and got ready for action. Simultaneously, one of the remaining gang members nervously reached for his gun. But before he could get a shot off, Anthony launched the donut. The impact of the mighty custard cream knocked the thug off his feet, hurtling him through a window.

Another gang member stumbled forth, pulling a shot gun out of his sock; perhaps he meant to use it, or perhaps it was causing him too much discomfort when he walked. Regardless, Anthony easily beat him to the draw. He struck him in the leg with a projectile chocolate-filled croissant. The young delinquent dropped the shotgun and collapsed to the ground. Clasping his wounded leg, he cried out in pain.

Shooting glances back and forth, ready for more action, Anthony realized he had successfully cleared the donut store of most of the devious motorcycle gang members. Just to be on the safe side, he hurtled a few donuts out the door, in an effort to completely scare off the fleeing gang members and feed any hungry squirrels that might be scampering around outside.

Relaxing his guard, Anthony surveyed the donut store once

more. He noticed that the counter person had taken cover during the donut onslaught. The gang leader still writhed on the floor, a large blueberry stain on his shirt. The gang member who was struck down with a chocolate croissant was squirming towards the shotgun he had dropped. Anthony raced towards him. When he saw the box of donuts clenched in Anthony's hand, he froze in fear and didn't attempt to grasp the shotgun.

"Do you know what this is?" Anthony asked, pointing the box of donuts at him in a menacing fashion. "This is the most powerful box of donuts in the world - it could blow your head clean right off. It did have six donuts in it," Anthony paused, "but in all of this excitement, I can't remember if I used all six of them, or just five of them. But just one donut is all it takes. What you have to ask yourself now is - do you feel lucky?"

The gang member didn't answer. Sweat rolled down his brow. He eyed the shotgun nervously, the box of donuts pointed down at him.

"Well do you, punk?"

The tension proved to be too much. The gang member decided, rightly so, to back away from the shotgun. Anthony kicked the gun away, but he wasn't going to let him off that easily. Pointing the donut box, he slowly raised the lid. The gang member closed his eyes, inhaled deeply and silently prayed for mercy. After a period of silence that seemed like an eternity, he had to know his fate. Opening his eyes slowly, he exhaled. The donut box was *completely empty*.

Anthony figured that he'd learned his lesson. He lowered his donut box and proceeded to leave. Before he passed through the door, he turned back to the gang member, still nursing his injured leg.

"You were lucky that I only had a half-dozen donuts in this box," Anthony began, "because I could have easily bought a full dozen - for a few dollars more."

Anthony Has Some Fun

For some people, fun is an acquired taste. For Anthony Zen, however, fun is something he has enjoyed regularly since childhood. Whether it be breakfast, lunch, supper or a late night craving, Anthony always enjoyed a heaping plateful of fun. In fact, he had giant buckets of fun delivered to his doorstep on a regular basis - and for discount prices! Of course, every once in a while, Anthony would grow tired of having fun, so he'd have some boredom instead. But boredom had its drawbacks. It had to be imported at great cost. With this in mind, and considering his meagre wages, Anthony could rarely afford the luxury of boredom.

All things considered, Anthony decided to go back to having some fun. He sat in front of the solitary window in his stylishly squalid flat and gazed down, three stories, to the busy streets below. He thoroughly enjoyed watching people carry out their daily duties and rushing off to work. Sometimes, just for fun, Anthony would actually show up for work himself. But today was not to be the case. With his head out the window, he inhaled the rich, satisfying aroma of exhaust, asphalt, oil, urine and barbecued sausages that rose up from the city streets.

It suddenly dawned on Anthony that something was missing. Rubbing his chin, he looked up at the sky. He shot a glance to his left, to his right. Blocks of flats and office towers everywhere. Nothing unusual. So why did he think something was out of place? He twisted around in his chair. His flat seemed in order, but something was definitely wrong. He poked his head out the window, as far as possible, and looked straight down. On the pavement directly below, a man lay unconscious, a crowd gathered around him. Anthony snapped his fingers and nodded knowingly. There was a small amount of dirt on his windowsill. That's what it was all along. He knew something was out of place. It didn't take a genius to tell that his potted plant had gone missing.

Anthony's realization was immediate. He leaped up from his chair. He was a man of action. Full of a sense of urgency, and determined to do the best thing possible, he raced into the kitchen and made himself a sandwich. Gobbling it down in record time, he felt drowsy. Returning to his seat in front of the window, he relaxed and watched the clouds roll overhead. He could have fallen asleep there, if it was not for Monty's interference.

Monty snored on and off, quite loudly. Every time he snored, he issued a loud ringing sound. The ringing was so authentic that Anthony was fooled into racing over to answer his telephone. But he was too ingenious to be tricked by his cat. After running to answer the telephone for the seventh time, he took the phone off the hook and let Monty ring all he wanted.

Returning to his seat at the window, Anthony wondered if Monty was dreaming – and if so, what was he dreaming? It struck him that this was one of the very few times that Monty was not watching him. Fast asleep atop the dresser, he had temporarily abandoned his vigil for the world of cat dreams. Anthony watched him breathe in and out, ringing on and off. The cat was a complete mystery to him. The cat never did what he was told and carried on regardless. There was no controlling this sentinel quietly watching over Anthony's adventures – and one was about to happen.

"Now is the time for fun!" Anthony rubbed his hands together, sensing he was somehow free from obligation. When the cat's away, Anthony will play.

Anthony figured he was much more intelligent than his cat, because he was taller and better dressed. His cat rarely wore anything at all! But more importantly, Anthony figured he was more advanced since he could not eat cat food and enjoy it. Although he had tried cat food on three or four occasions, he did not care for it and chose never to eat it again. In his mind, mankind's ability to choose other food items over cat food placed them above the intellectual standing of the feline race whose descendants seemed satisfied with its taste.

Never one to let taxing intellectual pursuits interfere with the enjoyment of such a wondrous day, Anthony erased all thoughts of Monty. Returning his gaze to the street far below, he noticed that several police officers had joined the growing crowd, surrounding the unconscious man. Some of the police officers were busy collecting pieces of broken pottery, placing them in clear plastic bags. Others, with pen and paper in hand, nodded continually as onlookers stepped forward and pointed up towards Anthony's block of flats.

"What a curious bunch," Anthony shook his head, wishing he

knew what they were saying.

He thought it possible that the police were initiating a 'clean up the city pavements' program, coupled with an attempt to get crowds of tourists to appreciate local architecture. However, he did not know why they chose *his* block of flats; it wasn't very interesting, or historic, as far as he was concerned. Regardless, he could not argue that the pavement in front of his building needed to be cleaned up. With all the broken pottery and unconscious people littering the streets, it was obvious that something had to be done. He admired the local authorities for their tenacity and dedication.

Inhaling once more that exotic combination of exhaust, asphalt, oil, urine and barbecued sausages that should be bottled and sold as 'City', Anthony's attention drew away from the crowd gathering below him. Looking further up the street, beyond the crowd, he sat forward in his seat, neck craned. He had spotted a postman, slowly making his way towards his building. So far below him, the postman appeared quite small, yet his uniform and mail bag distinguished him from everyone else on the city streets. As he drew closer, weaving through the gathered crowd, Anthony could see every detail of his dress. A neatly pressed uniform, sparkling buttons, prestigious hat, immaculate black shoes, a bulging mail bag. The postman appeared to be punctual, diligent and unafraid of dogs.

Anthony watched closely as the postman pushed his way through the crowd and stopped below him. Standing over the unconscious man, still sprawled across the pavement, the postman reached into his bag. Digging through the contents for quite some time, he pulled out a large brown envelope. Checking the address carefully, he leaned over the man and let the envelope drop onto his chest. He asked one of the police officers to sign for it. Anthony watched the other officers drop what they were doing and come racing over, knocking over a spectator or two. They seemed to be inquiring if their pay cheques had arrived.

Shaking his head and waving his arms in the air, the postman tried to pry away from the officers and make his way through the crowd at the same time. Breaking through the crowd, he was about to cross the street when Anthony became playful.

"Jump up through my window," Anthony thought aloud, laughing at the spontaneity of his own absurd thoughts.

Being high spirited and in search of fun, Anthony had really caught himself off guard. He couldn't stop laughing. It was a memorable moment, yet it was not exactly the sort of thing you could share with friends and have them appreciate it, let alone understand it. Tears rolling down his cheeks, he gasped for breath amidst fits of laughter. Catching a glimpse of the street below, the laughter immediately ceased. It was a sobering sight, filling him full of wonderment - and an odd sense of fear.

The postman was looking up at him - *directly at him*. There was no doubt about it - but why? Anthony became flushed. There was no way the postman could have heard his playful request. He was too far up from the busy street to be heard by anyone. Yet the postman, making his way to the other side of the street, kept his eye on Anthony, framed in his window. He definitely knew Anthony was up there.

The postman stopped on the opposite curb, his hand shielding his eyes from the sun, looking up towards Anthony. Anthony was completely captivated by the postman. For the life of him, he didn't know the reason behind all of this undue attention. He became even more alarmed when the postman leaped off the curb and began to race back across the street. Disregarding all traffic, he rocketed towards Anthony's building with great speed.

"What on earth is he trying to do?" Anthony gasped.

The rapidly approaching postman, although far below, made Anthony feel strangely uneasy. He could not explain it, but he was tempted to jump back and close his window; it was almost an unconscious decision. Somehow, he felt threatened. Somehow, he felt as though a serious mistake had been made on his part. He threw a quick glance around his flat. It all quickly became too obvious. It was too late now.

When the postman gained enough speed, he leaped up from the street with all his might. In a split second, he had bridged the distance between the street and Anthony's third floor flat. Anthony took cover behind a chair, just in time. Broken glass, splintered wood and liberated mail flew across the flat. There was a loud thud, as the postman crashed onto the carpeted floor.

Anthony remained hidden behind the chair. He was too shocked to face the reality of the situation. How would he ever explain this? Was an apology in order? To whom? Peering around the side of the chair, he watched the postman slowly pick himself up off the floor. The postman brushed the broken glass and splintered wood off his uniform. He removed his hat and played with it until it closely resembled its original shape. Sighing loudly, he began collecting the mail, which was strewn everywhere. He stumbled around the flat, as if in a daze. He could hardly get the mail back into his bag. After a brief struggle with a large package, he lost his balance and fell. He obviously needed help. Sensing that this was his moment, Anthony came out from behind the chair. He ran to the postman, stooped over him and punched him in the nose.

"What did you do that for?" the postman honked, clutching his nose.

"Look at this place!" Anthony threw his arms up. "Look what you've done! My landlord's going to kill me! How will I ever explain this to him?"

"Well it's not my fault," the postman looked Anthony up and down. "You're the one who told me to jump through your window."

"But I didn't think you'd actually do it! I mean," Anthony paced back and forth, rubbing the back of his neck, "It was so ridiculous, how could you take me seriously? How did you even hear me say it?"

"Never underestimate a postal worker," the postman shined his buttons. "We're very efficient."

Anthony helped the postman up, collecting his mail for him. He really had no choice but to forgive and forget. After all, if there was any blame associated with such an unusual occurrence, then *he* was to blame. The postman, being a dedicated public servant, was only following orders. Anthony guided the postman towards the door, where most people choose to enter. Showing him out, he watched the postman stagger down the hallway. Closing the door, Anthony sighed deeply. He sunk against the wall, looking blindly at the mess the postman left behind.

"Wait!" he jumped up, swinging his door back open. "Wait a minute!" he looked down the corridor. He saw the postman disappearing down the stairwell. "Do you have any mail for me?"

It was to no avail. The postman did not seem to hear him. Yet, he was able to hear a whispered request from three stories up. Anthony found it odd, but that's the postal service for you. Returning to his seat by the window, he was thankful that there was no troublesome pane of glass to contend with. Sticking his head out, he returned his attention to the crowd gathered far below. Apparently, a lot had transpired since the incident with the postman. The crowd was now enormous; the formerly unconscious man appeared quite alert. Still lying on the pavement, he rubbed his head. With police officers gathered around - notebooks in hand, yet still without pay cheques - the man looked straight up at Anthony's window and pointed an accusing finger.

Anthony's realization was immediate. It was inevitable. He knew what action to take, the best road to follow. Leaping up from his chair, full of a sense of urgency and determined to do the best thing possible, he raced into the kitchen and made himself a sandwich.

Anthony Goes to a Shopping Centre

Anthony Zen ran faster than a lumberjack who just realized he'd left his box of Raisin Bran back at the mess hall. It was freezing outside. The snow fell like yesterday's fish. Anthony had never been so cold. The unrelenting wind whipped around him. He shivered - not because he was cold, but because he suddenly thought about eating a fuzzy green worm.

Anthony wanted nothing more than to get inside the local shopping centre - to escape both the freezing cold and the insane bug-eating fantasies which everyone experiences at this time of year. Yes, it was winter time all right; what better place to spend the festive season than the local shopping centre? Anthony could think of no better place to waste his time and money. He was itching to get inside. He was cold. He was anxious. He was excited. He forgot to wash his hair, which probably explained most of the itching. He moved at such a speed that cars and pedestrians around him seemed like a blur.

Anthony raced past a group of firemen, huddled around a large campfire in the middle of the centre parking lot. He expected a smart remark from them - and he got it.

"Hey buddy," one of the firemen stood up, as Anthony sped by. "Where's the Raisin Bran?"

The firemen joined together in a good laugh, rubbing their hands over the fire, in an effort to keep warm. Anthony, ignoring the firemen, continued to rocket straight towards the doors of the shopping centre. He shot through both sets of glass doors. It immediately struck him that he should have opened them first. Picking himself up off the floor, brushing himself off, he shook his head to remove the shards of glass embedded in his hair. He pretended he was unfazed by the incident. He didn't want to attract undue attention; he was just glad to be inside.

Looking around, Anthony saw an endless sea of shoppers. They busily moved about, like a school of fish nibbling at pieces of crackers stuck between a lumberjack's toes. Just inside the doors, Anthony spotted an attractive young lady wearing a polka dot dress. She sat on a chairman, who was apparently fast asleep, while nervously gulping down a bowl of cereal. She seemed quite agitated. Now and then, she'd fire a glance around the centre, as if someone had been pursuing her.

Anthony continued on his way. He had no time for attractive young ladies wearing polka dot dresses who nervously munch cereal while sitting on a sleeping chairman. He had to buy a present. Yes, Anthony intended to buy a birthday gift for his mother - Mrs. Zen, oddly enough - who taught him to always use his head, except when hammering nails. He had a vague idea of the sort of gift he was looking for. He had to find something affordable. It had to be easy to wrap. It had to be something practical - something his mother could always use. It had to be something that would stimulate conversation at dinner parties; something durable that would last for years; something she could take with her wherever she goes. Of course, it would help if it was edible.

Anthony checked his watch; it was 9:00 a.m. Although he had the entire morning to search for a birthday gift for his mother, he felt rather rushed. All the other shoppers seemed rushed as well. In fact, the shopping centre was so incredibly busy that several businessmen were running around madly, dragging luggage behind them, angrily waving tickets above their heads. Apparently, they had mistaken the local shopping centre for the international airport. It was a strange sight, watching these enraged jet setters. Stranger still, some of them actually boarded their flights. Others were delayed at the entrance of HMV and forced to undress, because they kept setting off the security system.

Moving through the shopping centre, Anthony couldn't help but notice a startling social phenomenon. They were a distinct society in their own right - easily separated out, but difficult to study. It was thought they were simply the product of modernization, or perhaps inbreeding; no one knew for sure - no one dared get too close to them. They all shared several distinct traits. Most of them wore exceedingly bright coloured tops, brown polyester shorts, blue dress socks and white runners. They spent most of their time sitting on benches; although they carried just one shopping bag, apparently it was heavy enough that they had to sit and rest every ten feet. Quite often, they'd sit down beside you and begin to discuss the weather, or sometimes they'd scratch their ankles. Sometimes they'd scratch *your ankles*. In scientific circles, they're called 'shopping centre people' – or 'centre people' for short.

Of course, the centre people have offspring - centre children. They're stronger, faster and more resilient than the average child. They had perfected the art of running at great speeds, falling flat on their faces and yet still be able to leap right up and collide with some unsuspecting shopper. The centre children seemed genetically engineered to scream louder than any other form of wildlife on the planet. But their cries were only noticed by their respective parents. For example, a cry of 'mum' or 'dad' went unnoticed by everyone except the actual parents of the offspring. Some of the more advanced centre children, however, went against these hereditary factors. They had evolved the ability to alter the tone and pitch of their cries. As a result, they could get any number of parents to answer them, while their actual parents remained unaware of their whereabouts.

Amongst the flood of centre people, Anthony was surprised to see a lumberjack. He was a large man with a thick black beard, curly hair, rugged facial features, a gold earring and a tattoo of William Shatner on his chest. He wore a red plaid shirt, a green wool hat, suspenders, brown trousers and black boots. He was trying to count to ten, using only the fingers on his left hand. In his right hand, he held an issue of 'Psychology Today'; someone must have asked him to hang onto it. It was his strange behaviour that really caught Anthony's eye. He was running at full speed, often knocking down a few of the frustrated, luggage-toting, ticket-waving businessmen. He seemed to be desperately searching for something - or someone.

Anthony checked his watch; it was 9:00 a.m. He quickly decided to spend less time watching the people around him and more time searching for that perfect gift for his mother. Several stores caught Anthony's eye. 'House of Knives' seemed like the ideal place to get a gift for a loved one. However, recent tensions between the owner of the 'House of Knives' and the owner of the store next door, the 'House of Spoons', prevented Anthony from entering the establishment.

As it turned out, the owner of the 'House of Knives' insisted that knives were supposed to be placed to the right of the plate. The owner of the 'House of Spoons', however, insisted that spoons were supposed to be placed to the right of the plate; he called the owner of the 'House of Knives' a leftist pig. The owner of the 'House of Forks' sided with the 'House of Knives'; together, they banded against the 'House of Spoons'. The owner of the 'House of Plates' was caught in-between. Both the 'House of Knives' and the 'House of Forks' accused the 'House of Plates' of being a fence sitter - an opportunist, waiting for his chance to rule the dinner table. The 'House of Spoons' claimed that the 'House of Plates' were traitors who favoured knives and forks when beef was served, but would quickly side with the spoons when the pudding hit the table. Such mudslinging was common; however, the problem soon escalated. Violent confrontations occurred frequently, endangering the lives of unsuspecting shoppers.

The owner of the 'House of Knives' was a skilled knife thrower. It was said he could hit a man at thirty metres away - providing he was really fat. The owner of the 'House of Forks' was equally skilled with a fork. He could easily poke a man's eye out, or inflict a wound that, if not treated immediately, could become infected. The owner of the 'House of Spoons' quickly realised what a poor weapon a spoon made. Needless to say, he spent more time in the hospital than he did in his store.

Continuing with his search for the perfect birthday gift for his mother, Anthony felt fantastic, except beneath his right elbow - it felt dry and bumpy. He noticed the lumberjack stopping next to the indoor fountains. The lumberjack took his boots off and shook them; pieces of crackers began to fall out. Sitting at the side of the fountain, the lumberjack dipped his feet into the water. A school of fish quickly gathered around, nibbling at the pieces of crackers stuck between his toes. Suddenly, he leaped up, threw on his boots and continued running. He either had pressing business or one of the fish bit him.

Anthony checked his watch; it was 9:00 a.m. Time seemed to be dragging, yet he was desperate to find that perfect gift. One million gift ideas coursed through his head. He thought about clothes. He thought about gift certificates. He wondered if Abraham Lincoln had left the play early, would he still be alive today? Suddenly, Anthony was sprawled across the floor. Someone ran into him and their incredible bulk was pressing down on him.

Anthony was concerned about possible injuries. Were his ribs broken? Was his skull intact? Would his mother like flowers for her birthday? The person who ran into Anthony quickly got up off him and helped him up. Anthony was surprised that it was the lumberjack. The lumberjack seemed beside himself with worry.

"Have you seen her?" he pleaded, making sure Anthony was all right.

"Who?" Anthony wobbled, disorientated after the collision.

"The girl in the polka dot dress!" the lumberjack looked wildly around the centre. "I've been after her all day. She stole my Raisin Bran!"

"Wait a minute," Anthony looked upwards, rubbing his chin. "I have seen her! I saw her just inside the doors, when I came in."

"Take me to her!" the lumberjack cried.

He snatched Anthony up and flung him over his shoulder. Soon they were racing through the shopping centre. Anyone who got in their way was trampled. The lumberjack was angry. He was vengeful. He was extremely hungry. He was wearing too much Old Spice, which really irritated Anthony, but he was too scared to say anything about it. It was actually quite exciting for Anthony, riding on a lumberjack's shoulder; he only wished he had remembered to wear his trousers.

The wind whipped past them. The lumberjack's red plaid shirt flew open, completely exposing his William Shatner tattoo. People dove out of their path; others fell unconscious, because of the strong smell of Old Spice left in their wake. Anthony was tempted to start singing 'Roll out the Barrel' at the top of his lungs. The lumberjack handed him the issue of 'Psychology Today', which he was clutching in his right hand. He enjoyed an article on chronic bed wetting, before the lumberjack reached his goal.

"There you are!" he tossed Anthony off his shoulder.

The girl in the polka dot dress looked terrified. She was caught red-handed, with her hands in the cereal box. Dropping the box of Raisin Bran, she raced out of the shopping centre. The chairman, who she was sitting on, immediately woke up. He went over to the nearest telephone and contacted his office, to see if there were any messages for him while he was away. The lumberjack reclaimed his long lost box of Raisin Bran. Squatting in the corner, tears of joy rolling down his rugged features, he enjoyed a bowl of his favourite cereal.

"Two scoops of raisins in Kellog's Raisin Bran!" he cried, in

131

sheer delight.

Anthony checked his watch; it was 9:00 a.m. Although time seemed to be on his side, circumstance wasn't. He hadn't been able to find a birthday gift for his mother. He felt like giving up the search. Perhaps he had expected too much. He wanted the perfect gift, in every way.

"Impossible," Anthony thought to himself.

He was about to leave the shopping centre when it struck him. It was staring him in the face all along. He wanted something affordable; easy to wrap; something practical; something which stimulated conversation; something durable; something that could be taken anywhere; and it would help if it was edible. He turned and ran back into the centre. Shortly thereafter, he purchased a box of Raisin Bran.

Turtle Girl

While walking along the banks of a weed-choked stream, Anthony Zen noticed several things. In the far distance, an elderly man slowly made his way towards the stream - or at least it seemed he was making his way towards the stream. He moved so slowly that it was debatable whether he was actually moving or not. Dandelions were beginning to grow out of his shoes.

Beside the stream bank, a young couple played catch with their five year-old son. The father had a strong pitching arm, but the mother was a poor catcher. Each time she missed the boy, he'd let out a yelp as he fell to the ground. Other than that, he was generally well-behaved. The mother turned to Anthony and explained that her husband was throwing him too high; the sun was getting in her eyes, so she couldn't see him coming back down. Just then, her husband tossed the boy and caught her completely off guard. The young boy sailed over her head and landed amongst the cattails in the weed-choked stream.

The young couple searched frantically for their son, but he had become lost in the weeds. The mother called out to him. The father became quite upset; it was a lovely day and he wasn't ready to go home yet. All the young couple's efforts were in vain. Their son remained hidden from them. Maybe he had grown tired of playing catch. After all, family outings are difficult to plan; not everyone has the same interests.

After watching the young couple search for their son for a few hours, Anthony decided to help out. He was reluctant at first. Time was flying. The elderly man had advanced three feet forward. The dandelions in his shoes were now in full flower. Soon Anthony's entire afternoon would be wasted. However, a series of events unfolded that caused Anthony to ignore the growth of dandelions in an old man's shoes.

Anthony had been the first to notice it. His alarm immediately caught the attention of the young couple, racing to his side. They had no idea what it was. They were terrified, but too curious to run. Whatever it was, it was racing through the cattails at great speed. Back and forth, back and forth it went - a zigzag pattern.

Suddenly, exploding out of the water, it landed on the bank in front of them. The mother screamed, clenching her husband's arm.

"What is it?" her husband cried.

"It's a turtle," Anthony replied, knowing something about these sorts of things.

The turtle was eccentric at best. It had a predilection for racing up and down the stream bank, chasing birds. It would rub up against their ankles and play with pieces of string. The young boy came out of hiding and began to pet the turtle. The turtle rolled over for him; it liked to have its plastron rubbed. The mother scolded her son for hiding in the cattails. She removed the mud from his ears and nostrils. The young boy expressed interest in playing something other than catch.

It was the perfect family portrait: a young couple, their mud-covered offspring and their playful pet turtle. Anthony decided to leave them in their moment of happiness. As he turned to go, however, he felt the turtle brushing up against the back of his leg. The turtle's gentle motion filled Anthony with a secret longing. Instinctively, he turned around. He was shocked at the vision which stood before him.

She had skin whiter than well-kept teeth, hair and eyes darker than the mole on Anthony's belly. Every detail was enhanced by the fact that she was completely naked. The young couple watched in amazement. The mother covered her son's eyes. The elderly man was still approaching in the distance. The dandelions in his shoes were beginning to sprout seeds. The turtle was nowhere to be seen.

Anthony couldn't resist the temptation. He leaned forward and kissed the naked beauty on her right shoulder.

"My, aren't you fresh," she stepped back.

"I'm sorry," Anthony quickly apologized, turning red. "I've forgotten my manners."

The naked beauty noticed that Anthony wasn't wearing any trousers.

"You're a strange one," she laughed, brushing a colourful fly from her left breast.

"I find you rather interesting," Anthony quickly admitted. "Would you like to go out for coffee?"

She suddenly became quite serious.

"There's something I must tell you."

"What is it?" Anthony felt defeated already.

She seemed unable to face him. Sighing, with Anthony hanging on her every word, she summoned the courage to speak.

"Between the hours of 9:00 a.m. to 6:00 p.m., I am a turtle."

"Well," Anthony paused to ponder the situation, "could I see you sometime after 6:00 p.m. then?"

"It isn't easy for me - being a turtle throughout the day," she began. "I can't expect anyone else to cope with it. Relationships have never worked for me."

Anthony thought about things carefully. He was genuinely interested in her. He wondered how they could make things work. How would his friends react when they found out he was dating a turtle? They'd probably think he'd gotten too mellow. Yet, it would be an interesting challenge; it would make for good conversation.

"Yes, relationships are a tricky business," Anthony began, hoping to reach some common ground with her. "They're rather like dragging a sack of potatoes to the top of a flight of stairs, opening the sack and letting the potatoes roll down the steps. Some potatoes roll all the way to the bottom. Some only make it half way. Some never leave the bag. And then some of them ..." Anthony paused and shook his head. "Come to think of it, that's a bad example."

Anthony realized that the naked beauty had ignored everything he'd said. She'd been staring at the elderly man who was still slowly, but surely, approaching the stream. Tears ran down her delicate cheeks. She ran to the elderly man and threw her arms around him. With great affection and care, she clipped the dandelions which were growing up from his shoes.

The young couple left with their son. Anthony decided to leave as well. He turned and looked back one last time. She was still embracing the elderly man, as the sun sank behind them. Anthony didn't know why she had left him for the elderly man. Perhaps he was a turtle in a past life. Regardless, as far as Anthony was concerned, little had changed. His potatoes weren't rolling and the dandelions kept growing.

Anthony Goes to Court

Anthony Zen had been driving around the city for a few hours, when he saw the flashing lights in the rear view mirror. He pulled over immediately. He had no idea why he was being stopped - no one ever does. He could only guess at how things might turn out.

"Do you know why I stopped you?" he imagined the police officer saying. They always used that line.

"Because you're a nutty mischief maker - a real leg puller?" Anthony would reply, in a burst of sauciness.

"That's right!" the police officer would howl. "Made you stop, didn't I? You fell for my playful little trick!"

But this was not to be the case. The police officer was tapping at the window. He seemed overly serious, maybe even angry. Perhaps he was having a bad day. Anthony rolled down the window.

"Do you know why I stopped you?" the officer asked.

Anthony refrained from joking.

"Was I speeding?" he replied, wanting to appear honest and helpful.

"No," the officer grunted, as though he wanted Anthony to keep guessing.

"Did I make an incorrect turn?"

"No," the officer shook his head, "that's not it either."

"I went through a stop sign?"

The police officer rolled his eyes and sighed.

"Is a taillight out?"

The officer crossed his arms and began to shake his head. It was obvious that he was rapidly losing his patience. Anthony became frantic.

"Did I run someone over?" he asked, in a state of panic.

"Step out of the car, sir," the officer ordered.

"I'm sorry?" Anthony replied stupidly, having heard the officer clearly.

"Out of the car!" the officer snapped.

Anthony did what he was told. He was terrified. He began to think that this had something to do with the fact he was driving a stolen police car. The officer looked Anthony right in the eye.

Anthony was guilty - it was obvious - but the officer wasn't going to let him off easy. He was going to prolong the embarrassment - the agony.

"What's that on top of your car?" the officer asked, pointing to the roof.

Anthony turned slowly and looked up. He returned his gaze to his shoes, unable to face the officer as he spoke.

"It's a gorilla."

"That's what I thought," the officer nodded slowly. "What's it doing up there?"

Anthony glanced up at the officer.

"Eating a banana."

"And how did it get up there?"

"I don't know," Anthony shrugged, "I guess it climbed up there, or maybe it fell from a tree."

"I see," the officer nodded, looking Anthony up and down. More than ever before, Anthony wished he'd remembered to wear his trousers.

"I suppose you think it's perfectly legal to go parading through the city streets with a gorilla on the roof of your car," the officer crossed his arms.

"I don't know," Anthony shrugged. "It was never mentioned during driver's training."

"Well, it isn't legal!" the officer snapped. "I'm going to have to take you down to the station."

Seated in the back of the police officer's cruiser, Anthony felt cheated. He didn't know the gorilla. He hadn't offered the gorilla a ride - the gorilla definitely wasn't a member of his car pool - yet he was being held accountable for the gorilla's actions. While Anthony was being rushed to a jail cell, the gorilla was sitting comfortably atop his car, enjoying a banana. The fact that Anthony had stolen the car - a police car, at that - was secondary to the fact that the gorilla had knowingly made a public spectacle of himself at Anthony's expense. If the gorilla had taken the bus, this miscarriage of justice would never have occurred.

It wasn't long before Anthony's day in court arrived. It seemed that justice would prevail after all, although no one really knew what the charge would be - not even the judge. Regardless, the gorilla was the defendant. He had just taken the stand when Anthony was awakened by his lawyer. The gorilla played it cool. He didn't answer any questions. He made no comments whatsoever. He didn't even take the oath; he was too busy scratching himself. At one point, during intense questioning, he made a noise of some sort; but the judge dismissed it as a simple passage of gas and ordered it stricken from the records. The jury was puzzled, but they admired the gorilla's tenacity.

The gorilla seemed so sure of his innocence that the judge let him step down from the stand. Anthony became angry when he learned that the gorilla was probably going to escape all charges. The decision would be based solely on the rule that silence is golden; therefore, the gorilla must be nothing less than a model citizen. Anthony wished to argue that the gorilla's lack of communication was not due to innocence, but as a result of evolution bestowing him with mental capabilities far below those needed to understand complex judicial methodology. However, Anthony decided to forgo that line of attack, because he didn't even understand his own argument, let alone the judicial system.

The judge called for Anthony to step forward. Anthony's lawyer was frantic. He told Anthony that their case against the gorilla was in jeopardy. The gorilla had become a favourite of the jurors; even the judge was fond of him. The only way Anthony could escape being charged himself was to humour the judge and jurors and act like a gorilla.

Anthony had nothing to lose and even less to gain. Playing the role for all it was worth, he raced towards the stand on all fours and leaped up over the railing. The jury was both confused and excited by Anthony's display. Most of them thought he was supposed to be some sort of squirrel. The rest of them were fast asleep. Even the judge was becoming weary. He had to keep banging his gavel just to keep himself awake.

It was obvious that Anthony had to act fast to maintain attention and win his case. He leaped up into a coconut tree, which happened to be right next to the witness stand. Swinging back and forth, he refused to take an oath or answer any questions whatsoever. He would only bare his teeth and shake his head violently, as if his ears were full of tics. The jury still thought he was supposed to be some sort of squirrel, but at least they were all paying attention now.

With a bang of his gavel, the judge brought an abrupt end to the proceedings. Anthony was given the lesser charge of public mischief. Anthony's lawyer patted him on the back. His impersonation of a squirrel had earned him high points with the jurors - just enough to beat the rap. Yet, on the way out of the court house, Anthony became philosophical about his lesser charge.

"Public mischief?" he wondered out loud. "If a mother could charge her son with public mischief, I would've been in the electric chair before the age of five!"

Yet Another Day at Work

Anthony Zen had just commenced his daily duties when he immediately made a pledge.

"I shall not look at my watch until the end of the day," he stood up, hand over heart. With his hand over his heart, he thought he detected an irregular heartbeat. Clasping his wrist, he checked his pulse. Counting beats, he looked at his watch and ...

"Damn," Anthony shook his head. "This won't do."

Anthony commenced his work again and made his pledge again.

"I shall not look at my watch until the end of the day," he stood up, hands behind his back.

Just then, Miss Java came by, collecting employee measurements for the new company sweatshirts. They were handsome white shirts with 'WORT' written across the front in bold, black letters. It was supposed to say 'WORK' but there was a misunderstanding at the printers and Anthony's boss was too cheap to send them all back.

"Anthony," Miss Java began, pen and notebook in hand. "How tall are you?"

Anthony checked his watch.

"Six foot two," he replied, suddenly realizing his mistake.

"Thank you!" Miss Java chimed, moving onto the next fashion victim, while Anthony sunk into his chair.

Anthony slowly banged his head on his desk. Obviously, this was going to be more difficult than he originally thought. He felt something on his forehead; it was covered with bits of paper and pencil shavings – the result of his labours. Anthony couldn't have that. He had to look his best at all times. He tried to remove as much as he could; however, he did not have a mirror to check his progress. Thinking quickly, he used his watch as a reflective surface and he ...

The pledge wasn't really working out. It cleaned out its desk, grabbed its coat, picked up a week's salary and headed down to the local pub to commiserate with other failed pledges. Drunken pledges would be haunting the streets for hours afterwards. Regardless, Anthony thought the pledge was a good idea. He theorized that watching the time too carefully causes it to slow down. Take for instance microwave time. It's a special sort of time, since for each minute you watch something cook, the cooking time is increased by two minutes - it's a scientific fact! Since Anthony's shift was a gruelling three minutes long - two minutes too long, for his liking - he did not want his working day to seem any longer than it already was. What could he do about it? And then it struck him.

"A-ha," Anthony exclaimed. He found their CD 'Hunting High and Low' in his desk drawer. He had been hunting high and low (no pun intended) for it for weeks now; he liked that 'Take On Me' song. They were, by far, the best of all the Norwegian synthpop bands, a field that was ripe for competition.

"A-ha!" Anthony cried, even louder.

"You finally found that CD?" Meathead hollered, looking towards Anthony.

"No," Anthony replied. "I have an idea this time!"

Anthony removed his watch and put it in his desk drawer, right next to his treasured CD. Now he was ready. His pledge was back; it smelt like it had been having a conversation with Jack Daniels, but it was back nonetheless.

With his drunken pledge hovering next to him, Anthony could not concentrate on his work. The unsharpened pencils, and unshuffled papers, were beginning to pile up. He kept wondering what time it was. The temptation to look at his watch became stronger than the smell of rotten fish at the back of a Mexican bus. He needed a distraction, to take his mind off the time of day – and fast!

Anthony looked over to Miss Java, to see what she was up to. The steam, billowing up from her various coffee pots and kettles, did wonders for her complexion. She looked better than ever. Her face reminded Anthony of a playful kitten trapped inside a small pumpkin. Her eyes reminded him of a drunken fisherman casting out his nets. Her smile reminded him of a really clean pair of feet. Her teeth reminded him of small pieces of chalk. Sometimes, Miss Java would pluck out a tooth and sketch something on the blackboard. Sometimes, she'd pluck out two teeth, so Anthony could join her in a game of noughts-and-crosses. But not today. Miss Java, noticing Anthony staring at her, hurtled a handful of fresh coffee beans, striking him on the side of the head. Now he was definitely wide awake. There was nothing like fresh coffee to make him more alert in the morning; it helped sober up his pledge too.

Anthony glanced over at Meathead's desk. He rarely looked to Meathead for anything, but he was desperate. Meathead, noticing Anthony's attention, stood up.

"I'm not sure about this shirt," Meathead said, modelling the company's new shirt. "Won't people think I have warts?"

"That's 'wart'," Anthony explained. "Not 'wort'."

Meathead stood silently. His eyes moved slowly back and forth. Anthony, sensing his vague explanation was partially to blame, spoke up.

"People can get warts and those warts are spelled with an 'a'," he said.

"What's this 'wort' then?" Meathead asked, looking down at his shirt.

"Wort is a sweet, brown liquid that comes from milling, mashing and boiling grains," Anthony began. "It is an unfermented infusion of malt that supplies a growth medium for yeast which, via fermentation, produces beer."

Meathead looked at his shirt for a minute – maybe longer. Anthony's sober pledge kept him from knowing exactly how long.

"Is that a good thing to have on a shirt?" Meathead ventured.

"I'm not sure," Anthony said, heading back to his desk.

Anthony returned to his pencil sharpening and paper shuffling. Before long, he was in desperate need of another distraction - before it was too late! He began to daydream about laundry. He visualized it tumbling round and round in a clockwise fashion.

"No, no," Anthony interrupted his thoughts, shaking his head. "That won't do!"

He quickly imagined walking through the city park at night. The wind rushed through the trees. The leaves produced a ticking sound. In the centre of a flower garden was a large sun dial. A passer-by asked him for the time. As the sun rose, a rooster cried out. In the distance, the bells of a clock tower rang out.

"It's no use!" Anthony shrieked, stamping his feet.

His watch suddenly seemed like a parasite threatening to explode from his desk drawer, attach to his wrist and drag him down. He was becoming a nervous wreck. The suspense was killing him.

His pledge took two paracetamol with water. He could hardly resist the temptation now. There seemed to be no escape. If he did not act soon, he would end up looking at his watch. His pledge was reading a magazine. Anthony was out on a limb – all alone.

Suddenly, a plan developed. It would be Anthony's final option. If he didn't execute it immediately, all would be lost. Without another thought, he leaped up onto his desk, stretching his arms out as far as he could.

"I am an airplane!" he hollered, at the top of his lungs. "See my wings?"

Anthony managed to get the attention of his fellow workers. Even his pledge looked up from his magazine. However, Miss Java could hardly see him; the steam rising from her kettles fogged up her glasses. Anthony, still atop his desk, arms outstretched, began to rock back and forth, as if caught in a strong wind. He kicked paper and pencils off his desk, as though the power of his propellers had sent them flying. Thinking quickly, he created an authentic airplane noise, by forcing air through pursed lips. With arms still outstretched, he dove off his desk. Briefly touching down on the floor, he soared up onto an adjacent desk, sending everything on it flying.

Anthony's black, long-tailed dress coat, white dress shirt and black army boots made him a formidable airplane indeed. The fact he had forgotten, once again, to wear his trousers only added to the effect, as the wind raced past him.

Barney Blackfeet assumed a look of terror when he saw Anthony - arms outstretched, coat flapping, hair forced back - rocketing towards his desk.

"Shall I prepare an emergency runway?" Barney pleaded desperately.

"No need," Anthony hollered, above the sound of his propellers.

Anthony crashed down onto Barney's desk. The force of Anthony's brief landing scattered Barney's personal effects all over the office. Anthony dove back down onto the floor. He kicked over a garbage can, as if his landing gear had struck it.

"Your lights are on," Miss Java shouted at Anthony, after wiping the steam from her glasses.

Anthony thanked Miss Java for her concern. He immediately

turned his lights off; after all, it was not night time yet and he didn't want to waste electricity.

"Your landing gear is still down!" Meathead cried out. Anthony ignored him; what did Meathead know about flying?

After flying around the entire office, Anthony headed straight for Meathead's desk.

"You're coming in too fast!" Meathead shrieked, desperately waving two flags above his head. His 'WORT' shirt actually looked pretty good!

It was too late. Anthony didn't have much experience being an airplane. He touched down on Meathead's desk with such force that the desk collapsed; Meathead was nearly sent through a window. Luckily, Anthony escaped injury; he continued to circle the room.

Suddenly, Miss Java kicked off her shoes, leaped up onto her desk and stretched her arms outward.

"I am a cargo plane transporting coffee beans from Columbia!" she announced, with confidence.

She dove down and began to emit an airplane sound, flying around the room behind Anthony.

Shortly after, Barney was up on his desk.

"I am a F-15 Fighter Eagle!" he screeched, joining in as well.

Meathead was the only person left who had not become an airplane of some sort.

"I am a cargo plane carrying fresh meat to dinner parties everywhere!" he suddenly shouted, not wishing to be left out.

Of course, Meathead no longer had a desk to leap off of; as a result, he had to take a good run at it, in order to get off the ground. His first attempt was unsuccessful; he went face first into a wall. After several other attempts, Meathead was finally airborne, although he wobbled a bit.

The office was now alive with various airplane noises, as Anthony and his fellow workers flew around the room. Unfortunately, Barney quickly became the office bully; being a jet fighter - the fastest of the bunch - he continually threatened to shoot Meathead down. Anthony told Barney to behave himself, or else the other planes would join against him and force him to land. Barney quickly apologized.

Apparently, the airborne quartet did not realize how much damage they were inflicting on the office around them. Papers flew all over, chairs tumbled over, some of Miss Java's coffee pots were smashed, the wallpaper was peeling, a few windows were broken and the floor was covered with skid marks wherever they touched down. It was no wonder that the sound of airplane noises, breaking glass and smashing furniture soon brought the boss flying (not literally) out of his office.

"Anthony!" he screamed, somehow knowing he was to blame. "Stop acting like an airplane! You're getting everyone else all wound up."

Anthony quickly landed, followed by the others.

"I thought I told you last week to never impersonate an airplane again!" the boss scolded Anthony.

"I was a helicopter last week," Anthony interjected.

"Helicopter, airplane - I don't care," the boss continued. "Clean up this mess and get back to work!"

The boss went back into his office, slamming the door behind him. Anthony proceeded to clean up the mess, as Miss Java and Barney pretended to look very busy behind their desks. Meathead pretended he still had a desk. Anthony's pledge made a pledge to give up drinking for good.

Anthony had no reservations about what he had done. No doubt, he had successfully used up most of his working day. However, he did not know exactly how much time he had wasted. Keeping with his pledge, he refused to check.

Anthony Stays at Home and Sulks

It was a simply delicious morning. The sun blazed amongst the clouds like an enormous fried egg. Clouds gathered around it like streaky bacon. The gentle wind kissed the city streets, spreading butter across toast. Cheerful birds flew about like baked beans. Young people ran hand in hand into the bushes, with thoughts of love. They would emerge with assorted diseases, each easily treated with penicillin. Life was exploding from every corner, but Anthony Zen was safe from its shrapnel. He decided to remain in his flat all day, burning candles, while thoughts of plague, famine, taxes, crucifixion and getting his hair cut echoed through his consciousness.

Anthony was in a rather sullen mood. It wasn't often he found himself in such a mood. But every once in a while, something came along to upset him; such as a drastic change in the weather, poor TV reception or a petition signed by three thousand and forty-five people insisting he move to Iceland. There was no cure for his temporary displeasure with society's mundane workings, life's grim ironies and the universe's cruel humour.

Anthony's loyal feline flat mate provided no relief from the gloom. In the past, he found it quite delightful to listen to his cat's strange ringing sound - which no veterinarian, physician or professional cat therapist could explain. However, it was a chore maintaining interest in a ringing pet. To keep his cat interesting, and his guests guessing, he regularly changed the origin of his cat's name.

Was it 'Monty Python's Flying Circus'? A fair guess and a fan favourite; but no, not today – nothing that obvious. Was it 'The Full Monty?' An enjoyable, light hearted romp shedding much needed light on the little understood subgenre that is the British working class nudie musical – but no, not that one. Then *surely* it must be British Field Marshal Bernard Law Montgomery, nicknamed "Monty", who famously fought in both the First World War and the Second World War? Good guess – very prestigious, indeed – but no. Not that one. Not today. Today Monty got his name from *the* Monty. A largely forgotten legend. The greatest actor of his generation, whose influence can be felt to this very day. Like Monty the actor, Monty the cat would not be forgotten. He meant too much to Anthony. He was always there when Anthony needed him, giving him much needed respite from the chaos that was contemporary life. Anthony and Monty were inseparable. Together, these misfits would join the search from here to eternity to find their place in the sun - if you catch the drift.

Anthony pondered the full Monty *and* his flying circus. He enriched Anthony's life in so many ways. Monty was deceptively simple; Anthony liked simple things that actually meant a lot. It amazed Anthony that such a small, furry beast – just larger than a squirrel - could have such a hold on him. As a wise man once said: "Time spent with cats is never wasted." Anthony sighed. He would have liked to continue contemplating Monty's complexities but, as another wise man once said: "Time takes a cigarette, puts it in your mouth." Each cigarette was one hour of your life - Anthony learnt that in school. He couldn't afford it.

Anthony decided to see what was on TV – the opiate of the masses. He needed a fix. Hopefully, his dreary mood would drift away in a narcotic haze of adverts, chat shows and championship basket weaving. He turned on the television set and adjusted the rabbit ears. He did not know how the rabbit became stuck within his television set, but he was thankful for its presence. Its long ears, poking out the top, made for good reception. Sometimes, he'd feed the rabbit some carrots; however, the rabbit usually insisted on TV dinners.

To Anthony's dismay, it turned out that all the major networks were showing televised funerals. He thought it best to try something else to relieve his frustration with life and his deep, dark, brooding pessimism. He checked his cupboards; they were bare, except for a half-empty jar of Marmite. It must have crawled in there. Reading the ingredients, he noticed a warning label: 'WARNING – May Contain Marmite'. Whether or not the jar was half empty or half full was irrelevant; it was *Marmite,* for crying out loud – in his cupboard! Anthony disposed of the offender tout de suite - which he believed was French for 'sweet tooth'. He didn't know what Marmite had to do with having a sweet tooth, but that was France for you – always in the mood to play!

Left with no other option, Anthony sat down in his comfortable reclining chair, gazing at his collection of round objects, trying to ignore Monty's constant ringing. Oddly, the ringing began to fluctuate, creating a special atmosphere within the flat. The walls danced with gentle light, the sound rose and receded, fish swam over head, kelp softly brushed against Anthony's cheek.

Anthony floated up off his chair. The gentle current carried him along. He was drifting off to some foreign place – another dimension in time and space. He was floating through the dark, emerald depths of a Norwegian fiord. The cool water soothed him; it played with his hair and cleaned his clothes. As he breathed, bubbles escaped from his mouth; they tickled his face and caused schools of passing sheep to dart away. The sheep, hardened by life in the fiord, moved quickly through the depths. Anthony tried to count them, but it was too dark. Just then, a turtle crawled by with a burning candle on its shell. Taking it as a sign, Anthony picked up the candle and used it for illumination. The turtle looked at Anthony with disdain. She slowly turned around and began the long journey back from whence she came – probably to get another candle. Unbeknownst to Anthony, she would resurface in a weed-choked stream. Perhaps one day Anthony would recognize her in waking life, when the dandelions were the right length and the potatoes were rolling. But for now, Anthony was rather distracted with his new environment. The sheep swam freely around him, nibbling at the sardines and freshly baked buns that were attracted to the candle.

As the candle light illuminated the bottom of the fiord, Anthony noticed several things. Several vendors busily barbecued sausages, in case any customers should come strolling by. A postman walked up, checking the mail in his bulging bag. His buttons sparkled in the depths. He appeared to be punctual, diligent and unafraid of sheep. He gave the sausage vendors their cheques. He had a plaster on his nose. Must have run into a sheep, Anthony thought. When the postman looked up and saw Anthony, he assumed a look of terror and ran off, a trail of mail floating in his wake. Curious fellow, Anthony thought, holding up his candle to see if any of the mail floating overhead was his.

Continuing through the fiord, Anthony noticed a gorilla atop a police car, eating a banana. Anthony found that curious.

"Where do you get a banana at the bottom of a fiord?" he wondered aloud. Maybe a turtle brought it by. Anthony held up his candle and carefully moved it back and forth, so that the water did not blow it out. It illuminated shapes and forms that were strangely familiar to him. They were partially hidden in the murky depths, just out of reach of the candle's glow. Anthony held up his candle and slowly moved towards them. Curiosity may have killed the cat, but he was its willing passenger. He would cast light upon them. Suddenly, Anthony was awakened by a mysterious voice.

"There are no fiords in Norway!" the voice echoed.

Anthony sprang up, scanning his flat for the source of the voice. He blew out the candle and put it down. He was surprised to see a tall man wearing a wide-brimmed black hat, with matching cloak and trousers, seated on a giant egg in the corner of the flat.

"There ARE fiords in Norway!" Anthony insisted.

"No, there aren't," the tall man shook his head slowly.

Anthony ran over to his bookcase to find some evidence to support his side of the argument. He found books entitled 'Norway', 'Fiords' and 'Fiords in Norway'; he chose the latter in order to prove his point effectively.

Anthony opened his copy of 'Fiords in Norway' and began to read aloud about the schools of sheep and the deep sea sausage vendors. Convinced he had supported his argument successfully, he stopped reading and looked towards the tall man for his response.

"A-ha," the tall man cried.

"So you agree with me?" Anthony asked.

"No," the tall man pulled a CD from his pocket. "I just found my 'Hunting High and Low' CD. Been hunting high and low for it for weeks now - no pun intended!"

"I like that 'Take On Me' song," Anthony admitted.

"Good video."

"Great video," Anthony corrected him. "Moving from fiction into reality – heavy stuff!"

"They were, by far, the best of all the Norwegian synthpop bands," the tall man sighed.

"True," Anthony paused. "But that's a field that's ripe for competition."

The tall man chuckled to himself, slowly shaking his head, staring at his feet. Anthony was caught off guard, both by his response and the fact he wasn't wearing any shoes.

"So," Anthony began, getting serious, "Am I right about the fiords?"

"Anthony," the tall man looked up, still chuckling, his features somewhat hidden by his large hat, "my dear Anthony, how quickly you accept the absurd. Life is full of such random nonsense, yet you try to explain it using logic."

"I'm proud of my logical defence of absurdity," Anthony stepped forward, head held high, pulling up his boxer shorts, not really understanding what he just said.

"Anthony," the tall man waved his hand, "don't misunderstand me. I'm not saying it's a bad thing. In fact, I am here to compliment you on your efforts. I wish to give you credit, not criticism. I merely had to test your metal first, before I could be sure."

Anthony rubbed his chin. He was glad he was right about the fiords in Norway - a touchy subject, at the moment. He felt satisfied, but troubled nonetheless. His discomfort took the form of an important question, striking him like a train racing heavy thoughts towards a thoughtless station.

"Say," Anthony raised a finger, "who are you and how did you get into my flat?"

"Anthony Zen," the tall man changed his position on the egg, trying his best to remain comfortable, "Here we are - we're talking away. I almost lost my train of thought - racing between thoughtless stations, delivering their precious cargo and fining ignorance for having an invalidated ticket. All roads have led to this moment. It may seem trite, but I'll say it anyway - today's the day I found you. That is what counts."

"Needless to say," Anthony raised a brow, "I'm a collection of odds and ends. The train is approaching, but I'm stumbling away. I suppose I'm learning that life is OK. Is it better to be safe than sorry?"

"Odds and ends are needed," the tall man began; "they fill the cracks where perfection is unwelcome. And I agree – you can't stumble through life playing it safe all the time; you wouldn't learn a thing. This is why I have found you, Anthony. I have a very important message for you."

"Oh, the words that you say," Anthony shrugged. "Is this life or just a play? Will the train carry my worries away? What is this important message you speak of; do you have something for me to remember?"

"One day you will come to join us, Anthony Zen," the tall man nodded. "For we are a people ..."

"You'll take me on?" Anthony interrupted.

"Yes," the tall man sighed. "I suppose we will."

"I'll be gone in a day?"

"No," the tall man dead panned, growing restless. "Not a day. Not for some time. Now, as I was saying: we are a people who understand you - relate to you. You forget to wear trousers, we forget to wear shoes - that's what I call harmony."

"Well," Anthony interrupted, somewhat confused by it all, "in that case, we'll have a hard time finding a restaurant that'll serve us."

"Anthony," the tall man raised his hand, "do not concern yourself with the conventions of the modern world - besides, we can go through drive-thru. The key is to continue to lead your life as you see fit. Follow your dreams down the road. Look for the off ramps. Veer out into reality. Accept the unusual at every turn. Embrace the absurd at every juncture. Learn to live amongst seemingly meaningless, random events, but try to avoid being institutionalized. This is the meaning of life. It is up to you to get others to realize this."

"I'm not so sure about it," Anthony sighed. "How can we go through drive-thru? I don't have a car. We could maybe walk through, but you're barefoot and there could be gum on the pavement."

The tall man stared blankly down at Anthony. He switched positions on the egg, his bare feet clutching the smooth contours of the shell - trying not to fall off.

"The elders were right," he nodded, "you really are the man for the job. And they were wise to suggest that you join us."

"Join you?" Anthony perked up.

"Yes," the tall man smiled, "one day you will be called to join us, but not today. Instead, I leave you with this giant egg."

The tall man hopped off the egg. Pointing his finger towards a wall, moving it in a counterclockwise fashion, a dimensional door between time and space opened up. Anthony became worried. The last time a dimensional door opened up in his flat, his landlord gave him hell.

"I must leave you now, Anthony," the tall man continued.

"This egg is yours. Take good care of it, because whenever Cameron Straughan runs out of ideas, this egg will hatch and a new idea will be born. The idea will move from reality into fiction. The idea will carry you far from the norms, boundaries and restrictions dictated by modern life towards inner happiness. When others learn of your adventures, and follow your path, the idea will guide them from fiction into reality. In that way, you will teach others how to live. This is your destiny, Anthony. It is your gift to humankind."

Anthony stood speechless, staring at the tall man. After two awkward minutes of silence, the tall man spoke.

"Alright, look," he sighed. "It's an egg, for crying out loud! Just keep it safe. Do … not … break … it! OK?" the tall man started towards the dimensional door. Suddenly, he stopped and turned to Anthony. "By the way, I wouldn't recommend sitting on it," he gestured to the egg – "my back is killing me!"

The tall man tipped his hat, flung back his cloak and disappeared into the dimensional door.

Alone in his flat, with little else to do, Anthony proudly added the giant egg to his collection of round objects. As Monty rang on in the background, he felt secure that new ideas were about to hatch and he would gladly continue to live life as he always had.

ABOUT THE AUTHOR

Cameron A. Straughan is a writer, photographer and STEM teacher. His writing has appeared in several popular publications including 'Satire: The Journal of Contemporary Satire', 'The Dream People Online Literary Journal' and 'Black Cat 115'. He has performed his short stories at several open-mike events; including readings in Windsor, Ontario and throughout Vancouver, BC. His award-winning humorous films have appeared in many festivals around the world.

Photograph of Cameron A. Straughan by Christine Ashton.

Printed in Great Britain
by Amazon